Hell Squad: Reed

Anna Hackett

Reed

Published by Anna Hackett
Copyright 2015 by Anna Hackett
Cover by Melody Simmons of eBookindiecovers
Edits by Tanya Saari

ISBN (eBook): 978-0-9941948-6-2
ISBN (paperback): 978-0-9943584-0-0

What readers are saying about Anna's Science Fiction Romance

At Star's End - One of Library Journal's Best E-Original Romances for 2014

The Phoenix Adventures – SFR Galaxy Award winner for Most Fun New Series

The Anomaly Series – An Action Adventure Romance Bestseller

"Action, danger, aliens, romance – yup, it's another great book from Anna Hackett!" – Book Gannet Reviews, review of *Hell Squad: Marcus*

"Action, adventure, heartache and hot steamy love scenes." – Amazon reviewer, review of *Hell Squad: Cruz*

"Hell Squad is a terrific series. Each book is a sexy, fast-paced adventure guaranteed to please." – Amazon reviewer, review of *Hell Squad: Gabe*

Don't miss out! For updates about new releases, action romance info, free books, and other fun stuff, sign up for my VIP mailing list and get your free copy of the Phoenix Adventures novella, *On a Cyborg Planet.*

Visit here to get started:
www.annahackettbooks.com

Chapter One

"Moving in on the target now."

Reed MacKinnon kept his voice low as he murmured into his comms device. He crept forward silently on his belly, toward the edge of the roof of the ruined house.

Below, he heard a woman sobbing, a man shouting, and aliens snarling.

Carefully peering down, he saw the group of seven raptors towering over a human couple. The man and woman looked like they'd been on the move for a while. Their clothes were tattered and dirty, and they had a hungry, desperate look. And now they had aliens waving ugly scaled weapons in their faces.

Reed lined up his mayhem carbine. The weapon had a mini-missile launcher attached, but he wouldn't need that right now. Through his scope, he stared at one of the dinosaur-like humanoid's faces with its gray scales and red eyes. Nope, a good ol' laser shot to the head would be enough.

He waited patiently for his squad's leader to make the call. Reed couldn't see his teammates, but he knew they were nearby somewhere. Shaw would be looking down the laser scope of his long-range sniper rifle. Claudia would be silently bouncing on her heels, ready to rush in. Gabe would be a ghost, hiding in the shadows with his big-ass combat knife in hand. Cruz would be steady and calm, waiting for Marcus' command. And Marcus, he'd be gritting his teeth and pissed off, waiting for the right moment to hit these aliens and rescue the couple.

"Just leave us alone," the man below yelled.

One seven-foot-tall raptor kicked out with a huge, booted foot. He caught the man in the chest, sending him sprawling in the dirt.

"Don't!" The woman scrambled toward her partner, tangled blonde hair falling around her face. "You've taken everything. Our homes, our children, our planet. What more can you want from us?"

It was true. The raptors had come in their huge alien ships and annihilated almost all life on Earth. They'd ruined the cities, decimated most of the population, stolen resources. But there was more they could take. The real, hideous reason they were here. Reed's gut roiled. Freedom was every man's right, and these bastards had flown halfway around the galaxy to take humanity's freedom away from them.

Reed stared down his scope. Well, these humans weren't about to roll over and make it easy. The aliens were going to get a hell of a fight.

One raptor soldier snagged the woman by the collar of her shirt and dragged her toward the black, squat-looking vehicle covered in spiked armor plating nearby.

"Shaw, on my command, take out the patrol leader, then the alien next to him." Marcus Steele's gravelly voice rasped over the comm. "Reed, you take out the big bastard on the right. Gabe and Claudia, move in and take out the other three. Cruz, you can have the guy holding the woman. I'll disable their vehicle and driver."

Battle calm flowed over Reed. Another few tense seconds passed. The woman was screaming at the top of her lungs now and her struggling husband got a kick to the head for his attempts to help his wife.

"Go," Marcus said.

Hell Squad burst into action.

A single laser blast and the head raptor fell to the ground. Damn, Shaw was a hell of a shot. Reed squeezed the trigger on his carbine and watched his target fall. Then there was an explosion of movement below as the rest of the team swung into action.

They were so good. Reed felt a flash of pride. He'd been a United Coalition Navy SEAL before the alien attack, and the men and women on his SEAL team had been amazing soldiers. He'd thought they were the best.

Then he'd joined Hell Squad.

They came from a mix of backgrounds. Any surviving military members had been banded together into the squads that now fought back against the aliens occupying the ruins of Sydney, Australia—once the beautiful harbor capital of the

United Coalition. The Coalition was the result of the amalgamation of countries like Australia, the United States, Canada, India and some European nations.

Now Sydney was just burned-out ruins, shattered beyond repair. He didn't know about the other capital cities around the world, but it was a safe bet they were all in the same condition. He'd been on a diving vacation in Australia when the invasion hit. He'd spent months heading south to find what was left of the human military.

Reed watched Gabe move, faster than any human should be able to. The dark, intense man was a machine. He'd already taken down two raptors and beside him, Claudia—Hell Squad's lone female soldier—jammed her carbine against a raptor's chest and opened fire.

By the time Reed slid off the roof, the fight was over. Raptor bodies sprawled on the ground. Cruz was carrying a sobbing woman over to her husband, while Claudia checked the man's injuries. All in a day's work for Hell Squad.

Reed stared up at the sky. A thunderstorm was threatening on the horizon, lightning flashing in the dark clouds. Far in the distance, he saw red lights zipping across the sky, away from them, thankfully. It was a raptor ptero ship. He swung his weapon over his shoulder. He doubted the aliens would give up easily, but neither would the humans.

Reed would fight for his freedom, for the freedom of every person sheltering in Blue

Mountain Base—a military base buried deep in the Blue Mountains west of Sydney—until the day he died. He knew what it was like to have everything taken from you—even your dignity. And in the past, he'd seen fellow soldiers who'd been taken captive and suffered atrocities beyond comprehension.

No one had the fucking right to do that to anyone.

His gut tightened. He'd watched one of the best soldiers he'd had the privilege of serving with be rescued from enemy hands...only to never fully recover, living a life rushing from one bad decision to another.

Yeah, he'd fight these aliens, or die trying.

An image of huge brown eyes flickered through his head. He fought for her, too. For her to be free of the ugly memories of what the aliens had done to her.

"Aw, fuck."

Marcus' harsh exclamation made Reed glance over. His boss stood at the rear of the raptor vehicle with its back door wide open.

The squad hurried over. Reed glanced in and his jaw went tight. *Fuck.*

Humans huddled inside. Some were unconscious, sprawled on the floor. Others clung to each other, staring with wide, frightened eyes.

Jesus, some of them were just kids. Reed's hands clenched on his carbine. Fuck these alien invaders to hell.

"Get 'em out." Marcus pressed a hand to his ear.

"Elle, we have human survivors. Ten of them. Send the Hawk in to pick us up."

"Roger that, Marcus."

Elle Milton's smooth voice came over the line. Their comms officer was the last member of their squad. She fed them intel, raptor numbers and saved their butts when the fighting got too hot. She'd also taken on the mammoth task of smoothing out Marcus' rough edges.

"And have Emerson and the medical team on standby when we get back to base," Marcus added.

"I will," Elle responded. "Come home in one piece."

Reed caught a slight softening in the man's scarred face. Looked like Elle was having some success. Their fearless leader was so in love with the classy, young woman. Reed felt his chest tighten. Must be nice to know you had someone waiting for you.

"Hawk's here, *amigos*," Cruz said. "Let's get these people on board."

Reed looked up. For a second, he didn't see anything, then he spotted a vague shimmer in the air—it looked like a heat mirage. The shimmer changed as the Hawk pilot turned off the quadcopter's illusion system. The dark-gray copter rapidly descended to their location, its four rotors spinning. After its skids touched dirt, the soldiers began carrying the human survivors to the Hawk.

They loaded the shell-shocked people in, setting them in the seats, securing safety harnesses over them. As Reed helped the last person out of the alien vehicle—a slim, young man—he spotted something in the back. Something blinking. With a frown, he handed the man over to Shaw and climbed into the vehicle.

On the floor at the back was a small cube the size of his palm. It was black but glowed red intermittently. It looked a lot like the data crystals he knew the raptors used to store data. But the data crystals didn't glow. He picked it up. It had some weight, but wasn't very heavy, and it wasn't hot.

"Reed? What have you got?"

Marcus stood outside, his tough form silhouetted by the sun.

Reed held up the cube. "What do you think this is?"

Marcus frowned. "Hopefully not something that explodes. Elle? Reed found some raptor tech. Sending an image through now." Marcus yanked a camera off his belt and snapped a few shots.

Reed knew the drone Elle had hovering somewhere nearby would pick up the images and relay them back to base.

A moment later, Elle made a humming noise. "The pics are coming through now. Hmm, I think we've seen something like this before. Let me just check with Noah."

Noah Kim was the comp and tech genius who ran the base's tech team. He kept the lights on and all the electronics running.

"Bring it in!" Excitement rang in Elle's voice. "It's some sort of energy source. We found one before, but it wasn't operational. Natalya wants it."

Just the mention of her name made everything in Reed come to brilliant life. Dr. Natalya Vasin. Genius energy scientist. Beautiful woman. Alien torture survivor.

"Got it, Elle." Reed slipped the energy cube into a small bag on his belt. "Tell her I'll drop it off to her at the comp lab."

Reed imagined Natalya at her desk, wearing one of those fitted skirts and prim white shirts she seemed to favor. They always made him want to mess her up a little. *Cool it, MacKinnon. She's still recovering.*

Cruz appeared. "Survivors are loaded. Let's get back to base for a cold beer and a warm woman."

Shaw snorted from near the Hawk. "Easy for you, you have a woman waiting for you. Some of us have to work to find ours."

Claudia sniffed. "And you have to work extra hard to make up for your lack of personality and lack of stamina."

Shaw raised a brow. "Ha, look who's talking, Miss Snarky Sharp Edges. No one could get close enough to you without suffering cuts."

Claudia gave him an icy smile and shot him the finger before she bounded into the Hawk.

Reed climbed in, casting one last glance around the ruined suburb surrounding them. The storm was getting closer, the smell of impending rain in the air. He breathed deep and savored it. He was grateful to be at the base, but he hated being hemmed in. He breathed again. He missed the ocean, and the mountains—real ones, not what passed for mountains here in very flat Australia. The underground tunnels of the base and the recycled air kept them safe and comfortable, but sometimes he felt the walls closing in on him.

And he didn't have a warm woman to snuggle up to. As the Hawk took off, he grabbed a handhold on the roof. Marcus had Elle. Cruz had the lovely and dangerous Santha. Even silent, scary Gabe had managed to hook up with the base's smart, sexy doctor. Claudia was a frequent attendee at the base's regular Friday night gatherings, but if she had a special somebody, she was keeping it quiet. Shaw was the opposite, quite happily working his way through the single ladies at base.

Reed stifled a sigh. Since the attack, most people happily embraced casual sex. It was a way to celebrate life, stay sane, and feel close to someone. But while the offers had come in regularly and frequently, Reed had deflected them with a smile and a wink. He wasn't exactly sure why. He loved women, in all their shapes and sizes. Before the attack, when he was on leave, he'd always found someone to cozy up to. Usually some athletic type who loved the outdoors, like he did. But he never let it get serious—not when he could be shipped out to God-knew-where at any minute. He'd liked his life free and unattached.

But now—he fingered the cube in his pocket—now he felt a hankering for something else.

And unfortunately the woman he wanted wasn't ready for what he had to offer.

***

Natalya Vasin stared at her comp screen scrutinizing the data displayed there. *Hmm...* As she pondered the problem, she lifted the tiny photovoltaic cell from her desk. She'd pulled it apart, working on a solution to make it more efficient. Shaped like a leaf, the cell sat on disguised trees above the base, absorbing the sunlight, and powering the secret human haven below.

Since she'd been at Blue Mountain Base, she'd extended the daily hot water availability from two hours in the morning to all through the daylight hours. But she really wanted to get hot water twenty-four hours a day. It was her own private little goal. She *loved* her showers. Even more so after she'd been unable to have one for four long, horrifying months.

As her throat closed, she swallowed and forced the memories away. *You're in Blue Mountain Base. You aren't there anymore.*

The tightness eased enough to let air into her chest.

She turned back to her comp screen, and shoved her glasses farther up on her nose. She still wasn't used to the heavier black frames, but in an apocalypse you couldn't be picky. She'd lost her lovely wire frames in the initial invasion as the alien bombs had fallen. Thankfully, she only needed to wear her glasses when her eyes were tired and strained from too much time in front of the comp screen. She jotted a few notations on her tablet and read them again. Yes, that would help, and maybe give them another two percent output. But she knew it wouldn't be enough.

Then her gaze shifted to the tiny piece of amber glass resting on the desk.

The tightness in her chest returned and she purposely slowed her breathing. The innocuous piece of glass was an alien substance. From a tank used to trap humans...and turn them into aliens.

Memories rushed at her. The sounds of the raptors, the scary sight of their strange organic technology, the scent of their lab, the horrible sounds of wailing. Her own screams. Her hand went to her neck and she felt it...the top of the ugly scar that ran down her chest.

They'd experimented on her. They'd cut and hacked into her body.

And Natalya was no longer the woman she'd been before.

Before the invasion, she'd been a renowned energy scientist, and a guest lecturer at Sydney University. She'd been hired by energy companies to consult for exorbitant amounts of money. She'd been confident, certain of herself, normal.

Then the aliens had broken her.

No. She slammed her fist down on the desk, rattling the comp screen. She might be battered, but she wasn't broken. She'd regained all the weight she'd lost in the raptor lab—Doc Emerson had been forcing high-calorie meal replacements into her for weeks. She was working. She was being useful.

And she was damn well going to be normal again. She was also going to do her bit to fight back against the raptors.

Her gaze fell on the amber glass once more.

Preliminary scans had shown it was an excellent semiconductor. They might be able to use it, integrate it into the base's energy system and boost the supply.

Girding herself, Natalya made herself pick the glass up.

Up close, she saw tiny black striations running through it. They were irregular and looked almost like veins.

She picked up her hand-held analyzer and ran it over the glass. She studied the results, her eyes narrowing as she pondered the implications. Maybe, just maybe, they could splice thin layers of it into the photovoltaic cells. But she needed to run a lot of tests on it first. And needed to make sure this alien tech wasn't...alive and able to do damage.

The comp lab door opened and she looked over her shoulder.

Reed. She stilled, a slight tremble running though her.

He was still wearing the bottom half of his black carbon-fiber armor, but he'd removed the chest plates, leaving him in a tight, white T-shirt that stretched over wide shoulders and left muscled, tanned arms bare. His tousled brown hair was

HELL SQUAD: REED

streaked with gold. He radiated life and vitality, and the scent of him made her think of the sea.

His face was bold, with strong lines, and he had eyes the color of polished gold. A lion's eyes. That's exactly what she thought of every time she saw Reed MacKinnon—a healthy lion on the prowl for a sunny spot to lie in. Or prey to hunt.

Oh, and she'd do anything to be that prey. She was pretty sure the sexy soldier would be shocked to know the secret, X-rated fantasies she'd had about him.

"Hey, Natalya."

She managed a nod. "Reed."

"How are you doing?" he asked in his lazy drawl.

"Fine." She barely controlled the snap in her voice. He always asked her that, watching her with that patient gaze. She suspected all he saw when he looked at her was a damaged, fragile woman. He'd been the one to carry her out of that raptor lab when Hell Squad had gone in to rescue survivors. He'd been the one she'd clung to. He'd been the one to sit by her bed in the infirmary for days as she'd recovered. And he'd been the one who'd witnessed a few of her bad moments in the weeks that followed her rescue.

She wasn't damaged, dammit. She took a deep breath. "You're back from the mission?" *Oh, brilliant, Natalya, of course he was back from the mission.*

He tilted his head, watching her. "Yeah. Rescued some humans the raptors were dragging off."

To another lab, probably. Natalya swallowed the

lump in her throat. But, she reminded herself that Reed had blown up the alien's secret Genesis Facility where they'd been turning humans into aliens.

"I found this." He held up a black cube. It pulsed with a red light.

Oh. She jumped up and snatched it from him. "It's an energy source. I studied one that was damaged, but this...it looks like it's in perfect working order." She looked up and found Reed staring at her. "What?"

"Never seen you look so...covetous of anything before."

She felt heat in her cheeks. "You haven't seen me about to get in a hot shower."

Something flashed in his eyes and Natalya did a mental groan. God, had that really come out of her mouth? She'd never been this silly around a man before. She turned her back on him, knowing her cheeks were flaming now.

She set the cube on her desk and ran a hand through her short hair. Another thing she could thank the aliens for. She'd loved the long dark hair she'd once sported, but the aliens had shorn it off. At least it had grown back enough, and with a decent cut, the short style didn't look half bad.

Reed edged closer, his big body lightly brushing against hers. "So, you think the aliens use this cube as a power source? Like a battery?"

At that one tiny, accidental touch, she felt a spark of electricity skate through her. She tried to ignore his effect on her and focus on his words. "I don't know anything for certain. I need to study it more, but I'm hoping it could be an energy source we can use or..."

"Or?"

Their eyes clashed. "Something we can use against them."

His gaze sharpened. "Really?"

She shrugged a shoulder. "I don't know yet." Her jaw tightened. "But if we can, then I'll make it happen."

Chapter Two

Reed let Natalya's presence wash over him.

Her short, pixie-style hair accented her long, slender neck. All that creamy skin looked so soft. His hands flexed by his sides. Her brown eyes were large in her face, accented by her glasses, and her eyelashes were long and inky-black. God, he'd never noticed a woman's eyelashes before.

And her body...he was grateful his armor was hiding his body's response. Her plain white shirt was buttoned over her full breasts and tucked into a black skirt that skimmed over her recently-regained curves. Hell, those tight skirts and sensible shirts...not to mention the glasses, the whole package just made him want to lay her out and strip her naked.

He'd never had a secret librarian fetish before...but now he did.

He wasn't sure why she affected him like this, but she had, from the moment in the Hawk during her rescue when she'd clung to him. She'd looked up at him with such trust in her eyes, and in that chocolate brown, he'd seen a fierce will to survive.

She was smart. Way smarter than a grunt like him. And he liked that, too.

But Reed also knew she'd been through a nightmare. She needed time to recover and finish finding her strength again. He knew loud noises still startled her, she hated going to the infirmary, and sometimes she had trouble sleeping.

His gaze fell on the angry red scar just visible over the top of her shirt. His jaw tightened. It made him want to head back out and find some raptors to take down.

He cleared his throat. "So, you'll keep us posted on what you find out about this energy cube?"

She nodded. "Of course."

"You're wearing perfume," he said.

She blinked and touched the side of her neck. "Yes. Emerson gave it to me."

"I like it." He smiled. "Although, I like how you smell without it as well."

"I…smell without it?"

"Like cinnamon."

Her lush mouth dropped open and she stared at him. He thought he saw a flicker of awareness move through her chocolate eyes. He felt a corresponding surge of desire.

Dammit, what part of taking it slowly didn't he understand? "Natalya, I thought—"

The comp lab door slammed open hard enough to rattle the hinges.

"Lord save me from stubborn women." Noah Kim, head of the tech team, stomped inside and over to his desk.

With a genius-level IQ and hands that were magic with computers and electronics, Noah considered the lab his private domain. He sank into his chair and pushed his shoulder-length, black hair back. His Korean heritage was obvious in his lean, hawkish face. He reached back and snatched up two of the dice lined up on the shelf behind his desk. He guarded his little collection like they were treasure and now he rolled the dice between his fingers.

Natalya shot the man a small smile. "I take it you've been down in the detention area fixing the comp system again."

Noah crossed his arms over his chest. For a geek, he kept in good shape. Reed had seen him in the gym a fair bit.

"That dragon down there suspects we're all alien spies. God, and talk about workaholic, don't even think about taking a break or she'll ride you into the ground."

Reed swallowed a smile. "I take it we're talking about Captain Bladon?"

"Taskmaster Bladon, yeah." Noah tapped on his computer screen.

"You aren't going to mess with the ventilation in her quarters or something are you?" Natalya asked with just enough concern in her voice that Reed guessed it wouldn't be the first time Noah had taken revenge on someone.

Noah snorted. "She'd know it was me and come and make my life hell. I do *not* want her coming my way again." His gaze sharpened on the energy cube. "What do we have here?"

"An alien energy cube." Natalya held it up. "An operational one."

"Excellent," Noah said. "We should run some analysis tests on it, then hook it up to a power meter and see what it can do."

Brown eyes met Reed's. "Thanks for bringing it in, Reed."

"No problem." God, he wanted to touch her, but he clasped his hands behind his back.

"I might catch you at dinner later?" she said.

"Sure." Reed backed out of there. Before he did something crazy, like grabbing her and carrying her back to his quarters.

She needed time and he would give it to her...even if it killed him.

***

Natalya hovered in the tunnel outside the infirmary.

The new survivors were in there. Being cared for. Being assessed. And probably poked and prodded. Emerson seemed to enjoy doing that.

Natalya wasn't sure why she was here. These people had never been in a lab or experimented on like her. She pressed a palm to the smooth concrete wall. For some strange reason, she'd felt pulled here. So here she was, watching like a spy, her heart beating just a little too fast.

She should be back in the comp lab studying the energy cube some more. But she was running some tests and waiting for the results, so there wasn't much else she could do until they were ready.

She tugged at her skirt, and frowned. Since she'd gained weight back so quickly, the skirt was getting a bit snug. She'd have to visit the clothing store and see if she had enough clothing credits to get something in the next size. Luckily the business-style skirts and shirts she liked weren't popular in the base, so she didn't need too many credits. Most people wanted trousers, cargo pants, T-shirts—proper clothes for an apocalypse. She just wanted to feel a sense of normalcy in the craziness, and wearing clothes similar to what she wore before helped.

She heard footsteps and tried to look like she was waiting for somebody. Gabe Jackson, one of the members of Hell Squad, strode toward the infirmary. The big man seemed to fill the entire tunnel. He was about six and a half feet, with dark skin, a shaved head and a glowering expression. He scared most people.

But not Dr. Emerson Green.

The infirmary door opened and Emerson waved to someone back inside before her gaze zeroed in on Gabe. Her smile was brilliant as she launched herself at him. "Hey, big guy."

His reply was to snatch her up in his arms and kiss her.

Natalya watched them, feeling like a voyeur. Wow, the way Gabe held the doctor...and the way Emerson gripped his arms. Natalya was surprised she didn't see steam rising off them.

"Come on, you can buy me dinner." Emerson

linked her arm through his. "And I have a few ideas about dessert."

Gabe smiled. An honest-to-God smile that made Natalya blink. She'd never, ever seen him do that before.

Emerson suddenly noticed her. "Hey, Natalya. Were you wanting to see me?"

"No…I…no. I was just wondering how the new people were doing."

"Fine. Shaken up, but they're all right. My team's still checking them over, but apart from some malnutrition, they all appear to be healthy."

The infirmary door opened again, and a small group of tired-looking people were ushered out by a short, round nurse with skin the color of black coffee.

Emerson waved at them and watched them disappear around a corner. "Norah's taking them to have their quarters assigned. They'll just need a bit of time to settle in."

Natalya nodded. "Right." She stared after the retreating group. Her pulse tripped. Looking at them made her feel…nervous. "I'd better get back to the comp lab."

"Have a good evening." Emerson turned back to Gabe.

Natalya stood there a bit longer. Again, she felt that strange pull, an odd compulsion to follow the group of people. She fought it, telling herself to get back to her work. Then with a quiet curse, she started down the hall. After the group.

She followed slowly and at a crossways in the

tunnel, she saw the group turn left. Norah's voice echoed in the tunnel as she acted as tour guide.

Except one man didn't follow. He watched the group for a few seconds, then turned right.

Natalya frowned. He was slinking along like he didn't want to get noticed. Without thinking, she trailed along behind the man. He was slim, with dark hair, his clothes not much more than tattered rags. Where the hell was he going?

He rounded a corner. She followed.

The tunnel was empty.

Natalya spun in a slow circle. He'd been *right* ahead of her. How could she have lost him? All the doors off the tunnel were closed. She frowned, and absently rubbed a hand between her breasts. Her scar was aching.

"Natalya?"

Reed's voice made her jump. He strode down the tunnel toward her, all easy, male grace. He moved like an athlete, in complete control of his body. His hands were stuck in the pockets of his jeans and he wore a long-sleeved, navy-blue shirt that was just tight enough to show the ridges of his rock-hard abdomen through the fabric.

She licked her lips. A part of her really, really wanted to see him without the shirt. To have the right to skim her fingers over that stomach.

"Natalya? You okay?" He stopped in front of her.

"What?" She shook her head. "Yes, I'm fine. I was..." *following some new arrival for some unknown reason.* "I saw the group of new survivors heading to be assigned quarters. I think one of them wandered off this way."

Reed frowned and eyed the empty tunnel. "I didn't see anyone."

Natalya rubbed her scar again. "Strange. I—" Her words choked off as an ominous feeling rose up inside her. She felt a shiver snake through her, her muscles stretching tight.

"Natalya?" Concern threaded his deep voice.

"Something's...wrong." A lump formed in her throat. She could sense something, a threat, danger, hovering like a storm cloud.

Reed shifted closer...just as something fell from the ceiling and landed on them.

They smacked into the floor, the air rushing from Natalya's lungs with an *oof*. Reed's big body bumped into hers and he was cursing.

She raised her head. And looked directly into the glowing red eyes of the man she'd been following.

He hissed and swiped out with his hand. His nails were long and sharp, like claws, and they slashed her arm.

She cried out, scooting backward.

"Jesus." Reed bounded to his feet and shifted into a stance that made him look like a boxer about to head into a fight.

The man, raptor—no hybrid, that's what he was—snarled at Reed. Reed struck out with a fist, but the hybrid was fast. Really fast.

He dodged. Spun. And came straight at Natalya.

She didn't have time to scream. All she could do was raise her hands. He slammed into her, one wiry arm wrapping around her throat.

He dragged her backward, his arm tight enough to cut off her air. She coughed and kicked, her feet dragging on the concrete floor.

Reed followed, his big body tense and his face a mask of savage concentration. His golden eyes were glued to hers, urging her to stay calm.

Panic was rising, like hot bubbles in her blood. She'd been at the raptors' mercy for months. Now here was another one making her a hostage. She kept her gaze on Reed, trying to focus, trying to keep the wave of terror at bay.

Reed was here. He'd help her.

She tightened her grip on the hybrid's arm, trying to yank it away. A flash of anger stormed through her. No, she wasn't going to be a victim again. This time, she was going to fight back.

The hybrid dragged her through a doorway and into a darkened room. It smelled like dust and old things. In the shadows, she could make out rows of shelves, filled with neatly stacked items. A storage room.

"Let her go." Reed kept his voice calm but Natalya heard the dangerous edge in it.

Reed was always so easygoing, but at the same time, he was also a soldier on the deadliest command squad in the base. She knew he had to be lethal when he needed to be.

The hybrid hissed again but kept moving deeper into the darkness, dragging her with him.

She watched as Reed followed them, but then all of a sudden, the hybrid moved in a sharp jerking motion. He shoved her forward, hard. She smacked into Reed and as he caught her, they slammed into a shelf. Various items rained down on top of them and Reed covered her body with his.

All Natalya could do was hold on tight. He was so hard and big. Safe.

Finally, things stopped falling. They both looked up...just as the hybrid slammed the door closed.

"Dammit!" Reed released her and bounded forward. He slammed a fist against the metal door. Through a tiny window of glass, they saw the hybrid on the other side, smiling wickedly at them. His teeth were a little longer than a regular human's and jagged. Natalya shivered.

Then the hybrid smashed the door's electronic lock on the outside.

On the corresponding internal lock panel, the lights blinked off.

"No!" Reed pressed his palm against the pad. Nothing happened. "Fuck!" He kicked the door, making it rattle.

The hybrid grinned again, and then, while they watched, he climbed up the wall like a spider and scuttled off down the hall.

Natalya shivered and wrapped her arms around herself. "We have to warn people. He could..." The hybrid could hurt people, or do damage to the base.

Reed ran a hand through his hair. "I don't have my communicator on me. I'm off-duty. You?"

She shook her head. It was sitting on her desk in the comp lab. "Is there an emergency alarm button? We have one in the comp lab."

Reed's jaw tightened and he shook his head.

"They were fitted to the main areas and private quarters, but not in the storage rooms." He banged a palm against the door and yelled.

Natalya joined him. "Help! Somebody."

After a few minutes, Reed cursed. "We're too far from the main areas. No one will hear us down here." He ran a hand through his hair. "We don't have a lot of options."

She scanned the dark room. "There might be something we can use to break out of here. We should check."

He nodded. As they moved away from the door, the darkness got deeper. Natalya studied the shelves and she stilled.

Treasure. The shelves were filled with paintings, statues, old jewelry. It looked like the contents of a museum. She turned and saw more paintings stacked against the wall. "History."

Reed looked over. "What?"

She ran a hand over the statue of a sinuous woman. "Human history. This is all we have left of it. We've lost so much."

He moved closer. She felt the heat emanating off him.

"They're just things." His voice was low and deep. "People are what matter. Once we send these aliens packing, we'll make new history."

His optimistic view cheered her. She looked up at the bold lines of his handsome face and wondered, just for a second, what it would be like to be normal again. To have her once-solid confidence back. If she had it, she'd do what she wanted to do—seduce Reed MacKinnon.

Natalya's hand fell away from the statue. But she wasn't that woman, not anymore. Some days she despaired that who she'd been before would never return. And Reed deserved more than a cracked shell of a woman trying to put the pieces back together.

She tilted her head back and something on the ceiling caught her eye. "Reed, look." She pointed.

He peered upward. "Ventilation grate. Leads into the vent tunnels."

A way out.

"Can you lift me up?" she asked.

Chapter Three

Reed wasn't quite sure how he ended up with Natalya's soft curves pressed against him. He liked it. But at the same time, it was torture.

She was gripping his biceps, one of her small feet resting on his thigh. He gripped her waist and helped her up. She set her other foot on his other thigh…dangerously close to his groin.

And a twitching cock that liked the way she felt and smelled.

"Not going to work," she muttered. "My skirt's too constricting." She waved at him to set her down.

He did. She stood in front of him, hesitated for a second, then straightened her shoulders and hitched her skirt halfway up her thighs. Slim, shapely, creamy thighs.

Reed's heart stopped for a second. Then it started beating again, now a hard bang against his ribs.

She glanced at him, heat in her cheeks. "I'll be able to move a bit more now." She gripped his arms again.

His heart still thudding, he hefted her up once more.

"I need a bit more height," she said.

He boosted her up higher and ended up with his face mashed against her belly. *Damn.* He was all-too-aware that the bare skin of her thighs was only inches away. He tried counting to ten. Then twenty. He heard her reaching up, muttering under her breath in what he guessed was Russian.

Yes. A distraction. "So, your family's Russian?"

"My father was. My mother was French."

"How'd they meet?"

"On the New Moscow Space Station. Dad was an astronaut and my mother a scientist up there conducting experiments. They fell crazy in love, married and had me." She reached for something, and grunted. A soft, very feminine grunt. "We left Russia when I was a child and moved to Australia. My father took up a professor position at the United Coalition Academy of Sciences."

"So you grew up in Australia but still speak Russian."

"Only a little." She shifted again. "Mostly swear words."

"Do you know what happened to them? Your parents?"

She was quiet for a moment. "They were at the Coalition Academy."

Which Reed knew had been one of the early targets hit during the invasion. "I'm sorry."

"Thanks. And your family?"

"None left. Just some distant cousins. My parents had me late in life and passed away several years ago. I'm glad that they weren't here to suffer through the invasion."

A few moments passed. "I need a little more height. My fingers are brushing the panel but I'm not quite high enough."

He boosted her higher. "Put one leg on my shoulder."

Awkwardly, she moved until a slim thigh rested on his shoulder. "Ah, I'm not sure this is a great idea."

He could see her panties. And under that neat black skirt, she was wearing pink lace. Reed went stiff as a board. In more places than one. He practically had his head buried between her thighs. "Just get it done."

"Maybe I should try climbing the shelves?"

He gritted his teeth. "They're temporary and pretty flimsy. Just get it done, Natalya."

"All right," she huffed. She shifted around and tried to reach the grate.

Reed barely managed to stop a strangled groan.

Finally, she sagged back. "It's on too tight. Without a tool of some sort, I can't get the screws undone and get it off."

He nodded and slid her down to her feet.

In the process, her body ended up sliding along him until she was standing in the circle of his arms staring up at him with wide brown eyes.

Dammit. Control, MacKinnon. He stepped back from her.

Natalya stepped back, too. "All right, we need a Plan B. I will not let that hybrid hurt anyone. Let's keep looking."

Reed circled the room. The last hybrid that had snuck into the base had damn near killed Doc Emerson. They had to find a way out. He searched every shadowed corner of the storage room. Nothing. Apart from the door and the vent, there were no other openings into, or out, of the storage room. They were deep underground and past the cement walls he knew there were tons of rock and dirt. *Fuck*. "Nothing. We'll have to wait for rescue."

When she didn't respond, he looked her way. She had her arms wrapped around herself. He narrowed his gaze. She was shaking.

"Natalya?"

Her head shot up. Her face was pale. "I'm...okay."

"No, you're not." He moved over to her and gripped her arms. He expected her to be cold, instead she felt hot, a sheen of perspiration on her skin. "What's wrong?"

"Nothing." She tried to pull away from him. "I get these...episodes sometimes. I hate being...trapped. Locked up. Not able to get out."

Ah. It reminded her of the raptor lab. "Come on, brown-eyed girl, let's sit down closer to the door. There's more light there."

He sat with his back to the wall, knees raised. She dropped down beside him. She was still shaking and rubbing her chest.

"You're sure you're okay?"

"Yes," she snapped. "I'm not made of glass, Reed. I'm not going to shatter into a million little pieces or start weeping all over you."

31

The flash of fire in her voice actually gave him a sense of relief. "Good. Don't want tear stains on this shirt."

She shot him a look, but he saw the tension in her, the way her muscles were strung tight. Damn, he remembered those feelings all too well.

"Come here." He slid an arm over her shoulders and yanked her close to his side.

She made a small sound but slowly relaxed into him. After a while, he realized she was rubbing her chest, like it hurt. He wondered if her scar bothered her. She started to shake again.

He frowned. "Natalya?"

"Don't know what's wrong." Her teeth chattered together. "Feel...strange."

God, maybe there was something medically wrong with her, not just old memories. He slid a hand up to the base of her neck and started massaging. He felt helpless, there was nothing he could do to help.

But when she made a small sound and let her head drop forward, he realized his distraction was working. He shifted and put both hands on her shoulders, kneading her tense muscles.

"Better?"

"Don't stop," she said.

He kept going, letting himself indulge in the feel of her. Smooth skin, such a slim, enticing neck. He let his fingers slide up into her short, silky hair.

She let out a small moan.

Jesus. The sound shot straight to his cock and he shifted to try and ease his discomfort. The last thing Natalya was ready for was his needs. He was big, more often than not a little rough, and the things he wanted to do to her...well, he doubted he'd have much control when he finally got her naked.

She tilted her head back, her gaze drifting over his face. It settled on his lips and her own were parted.

Dammit. That mouth gave him all kinds of hot, dirty ideas. He closed his eyes and counted to ten. Twenty. Thirty.

When he opened them again, she was watching him.

Then she spoke. "I want to kiss you."

***

Natalya watched a mix of emotions run over Reed's face. Then his look turned hard and he took a deep breath.

"I don't think that's a good idea."

God. She'd thought...she pulled back. Of course, he wouldn't want to kiss her. He no doubt had a whole group of the base's pretty young things offering him far more than a boring kiss. Women with no scars, no dark memories, and a whole lot less baggage.

Be an adult, Natalya. "I'm sorry. Of course, you wouldn't want to kiss me. Look, forget I said anything, okay?"

He made an angry noise in his throat. "For a smart woman, that's a dumb observation."

"Excuse me?"

"I didn't say I didn't want to kiss you."

What? She looked up again, trying to work out what he was saying.

"I want to kiss you," he bit out. "So much it's fucking tearing me up inside."

Her eyes widened and her gaze dropped to his mouth again. He had a really nice-shaped mouth. "So...what's the problem?"

"You've been through a lot, I don't want—"

She shot to her feet. "I'm made of glass again." She flung out a hand. "You don't want to kiss the freak show and upset her."

He got to his feet now, and his tone lowered. "Do *not* talk about yourself like that. You're a survivor. A courageous, brave woman who lived through hell."

"But I'm too fragile to be kissed." Anger pumped through her.

"I want to give you time."

Right, he didn't see an attractive, normal woman, he saw someone he had to take care with. "You know what, I don't want to kiss you now. So this time, really forget it."

He grabbed her arm. "No."

"You can't have it both ways, Reed."

"You're punishing me for wanting to take care of you? A long time ago, I saw a soldier, a good friend, come home after being in enemy hands." He shook his head. "She never recovered. She rushed into things to prove she was okay..." He trailed off.

Natalya's anger dimmed...a little. "I'm sorry

about your friend. But it's my choice you're taking away, Reed. And I was only asking for a kiss, not for a life commitment."

He reeled her in closer. "God, Natalya. I want to kiss you. I want to do a lot more than that." He hesitated. "Just a kiss?"

Her blood ran hot, but she held on to her anger. "No, if you want to kiss me, you'll have to work for it now."

That made him scowl and amusingly, Natalya felt better. It reminded her how much fun it could be to have a man, one you could laugh with, play with, and fight with. She hadn't had much time for dating before the invasion, but she'd always liked sex. Really liked it. She missed it.

Reed was watching her steadily. "Natalya—" he rubbed a thumb over her lips "—I really, really want to kiss you."

She lifted her chin. His touch was electric. "No. Not good enough."

His hands slid up her arms, leaving goose bumps on her skin. Heat pulsed off him. He lowered his head, his lips a breath away from her ear. "Please."

She shivered. "No." The word came out breathy and lacked conviction.

His lips move into a smile. "Okay, how about this? If you let me kiss you, I'll take you swimming again."

Her breath hitched. "Bribery?"

"Incentive," he countered.

He'd taken her swimming once, when she'd had terrible nightmares and the base was closing in on her, making her feel trapped. He'd snuck her out into the darkness, and taken her to a small waterhole near the base. The moonlight on the water had been beautiful and he'd just sat on the edge and watched her swim and frolic like a little girl.

It had been magical. She definitely wanted to go swimming again.

She licked her lips, felt his gaze on her mouth. "Okay. It's a deal."

His mouth lowered slowly to hers.

It was a slow kiss. An exploration. He took his time, learning her mouth, sliding his tongue inside. Desire was a slow curl through her belly. Lazy and seductive.

She'd never thought Reed MacKinnon would be a slow kisser. She'd expected heat, a touch of roughness, a little bit of wild. Not this sensual slowness.

Oh, he tasted so good. She gripped his arms, her fingers digging into his hard biceps. She felt a tremor go through his body. His rigid body.

Realization flashed through her. He was holding back.

Disappointment was a bitter, bitter burn. She stumbled back. "You know what, I don't think I want to go swimming anymore."

"What?" Reed blinked.

Her hands clenched into fists by her side. "I told you I'm not fragile. I don't need to be handled like a china doll. I want to be treated normally."

"Natalya—" he reached for her.

She dodged his hand. "Tell me, is that how you always kiss? Tell me you weren't holding back for my sake."

His arm dropped and he just stared at her, jaw clenched.

She shook her head. "I thought so."

"I want to take care of you."

"You look at me and see something broken."

"You went through a traumatic situation—"

"I'm not broken!" she yelled. Her voice echoed in the small confines of the storage room.

He stared at her. "I know that."

"No, I don't think you do."

They stared at each other, the moment stretching out between them.

Then the storage room door slammed open. The large silhouette of a man filled the doorway.

"Reed? Natalya? What the hell are you doing in here? I heard shouting."

Marcus Steele stood in the doorway, clutching a carbine in his hand.

Reed stepped forward. "Marcus. A hybrid was among those survivors we brought in. He trapped us in here and took off."

Marcus muttered a string of curses and Natalya raised her brows at the creative...words he used.

"You're both okay?" Marcus asked.

"Yeah." Reed looked at Natalya.

She turned away to face Marcus. "I'm fine. But we need to find that hybrid before he hurts someone."

Marcus nodded, his scarred face grim. "There

have been reports of ransacked rooms." He lifted his weapon. "There's a bunch of us out patrolling." He yanked a large laser pistol from the waistband of his cargo pants and handed it to Reed. "Come on, we need to find this bastard."

Reed took the gun, checked it, and followed Marcus.

"I'm coming too." Natalya hurried out after the men.

"No." Reed frowned. "I'll drop you at your room. You lock yourself in until this is over."

Her last little hope of Reed ever seeing her as a strong, confident, attractive woman faded. And damn, it hurt. "I'm coming." She had to help find this hybrid. She wouldn't let anyone else be violated or hurt by these aliens.

She saw his jaw work as he ground his teeth together.

Screams and yells echoed from farther down the tunnel.

Marcus' face turned scary. "No time to argue. Let's go." He took off at a jog.

Reed shot her a fierce look, then followed his boss. Setting her shoulders back, she followed.

Chapter Four

Reed tried to tamp down his frustration and focus on the hunt.

Marcus was yelling into his communicator, organizing teams to run a search of the base. Reed listened in, all the while keeping one eye on Natalya. Damn, he wished she'd go back to her quarters and stay safe.

She refused to meet his gaze, and he cursed a few more times in his head. She didn't seem to realize keeping her safe was more than a priority for him, it was a driving need he had to follow. It wasn't that he thought she was broken or incompetent.

"Dammit, find the damn hybrid and quit wasting time." Marcus slammed his communicator shut. "Come on. We'll search the lower storage areas."

Where the hell would this thing go? What was it after? Reed pondered the questions as they jogged down a spiral ramp to the lower levels. This was going to seriously rattle morale. A part-alien loose in the one place people felt safe. They'd barely gotten over the fact that the aliens were turning humans, and that one had already got into the base before.

They entered another tunnel. One branch speared right, heading to the comp lab and the research areas. The other tunnel went left to more rooms that were used for storage. They were packed with scavenged goods—medicines, tinned foods, artifacts, clothing and electronics.

Marcus nodded left. "This way."

As Hell Squad's leader jogged ahead, Reed started to follow. Then he realized Natalya wasn't with them.

She was staring down the tunnel to the right. A strange expression was on her face and she was rubbing her chest.

"Natalya?"

She didn't respond.

"Natalya? We have to keep up with Marcus."

She ignored him and started down the right-hand tunnel.

Dammit. Reed wouldn't leave her. He hurried behind her. Had she heard something? He strained to listen for any sound, but the tunnel was silent.

He grabbed her arm and spun her around. "Hey. Talk to me. What's going on?"

She shook her head, her face a little confused. "I'm not sure." She rubbed between her breasts vigorously. "I just...we need to go this way."

She hurried off again. When she reached the comp lab, she went to press her palm to the lock, then gasped.

The lock had been ripped off the wall and

dangled uselessly by a few wires. "Shit." Reed lifted the laser pistol. "Let me go first."

When she started to argue, he shouldered in front of her.

"This isn't about you. I'm trained, this is what I do."

She stared at him for a second, before she nodded.

Reed pushed open the door to the lab.

Shit was everywhere. Bits of wire and electronics had been scattered from one end of the large room to the other. Hanging off comp screens and the backs of chairs.

And standing in the center of the mess was the hybrid.

He lifted his head and hissed at them.

In one hand, he clutched the glowing energy cube and in the other, the older, non-functioning cube.

"No!" Natalya pushed forward. "We can't let him take them."

The hybrid's demonic red eyes leveled on Natalya. He spat something in the guttural raptor language.

Reed shot at the creature.

The hybrid leapt, jumping high and crashing down onto a neighboring desk. A comp screen crashed to the floor. Reed shot again, green laser fire cutting through the lab.

The hybrid ducked this time. Damn, he was fast.

"Stay back," Reed warned and moved forward.

Where the hell had it gone? The lab was silent

now. Reed moved quietly past a row of desks.

The hybrid burst out from beneath a workbench, rocketing into Reed's legs.

Reed fell, but as he did, he aimed his laser pistol. He caught the hybrid in the shoulder and the raptor-human let out a scream and scrambled under a desk.

Reed rolled, got to his feet, and rounded the desk. The hybrid burst out from cover, running toward Natalya.

Spinning, aiming on the move, Reed fired.

At the hybrid's head.

Two shots and the fight was over.

"Okay?" Reed asked.

Natalya stood a few feet away, an office chair hefted over her shoulder, her gaze glued to the dead hybrid.

Reed suppressed a smile. "Don't think you'll need that."

With a nod, she set it down.

Reed strode to the hybrid and checked that he was really dead. With his body lying facedown and lifeless, he looked like a simple human. Reed snatched up the two energy cubes from the floor.

Natalya appeared beside him. Her gaze was a mix of horror and sympathy as she stared at the hybrid. "God. Poor guy."

"Here." Reed handed the cubes to her.

She took them, holding onto them tight. "He was after these."

Reed studied the small cubes. "Looks like it."

She cleared her throat. "I'm glad you were here.

I'm grateful for your help. I...I apologize for some of what I said earlier."

"Some?"

"I know you're a soldier, fighting and protecting people weaker than you is in your blood."

"But?"

"But you were holding back earlier." She brushed a short strand of hair off her forehead. If she had pointed ears, she'd really look like a fairy. "I won't accept that." She drew herself up. "Not from you, not even from myself."

That, he'd have to chew on later. For now... "How'd you know the hybrid was in here?"

Natalya blinked. "I...I don't know. I guess I must have heard something."

He frowned at her. He knew he hadn't heard a sound.

"You need to call Marcus, right?" she said walking backward toward the door. "And I need to work out what's so important about these cubes that the aliens sent him in here after them." She eyed the body again. "I think I'll do it in my quarters."

Reed watched her go, his gut churning. He didn't know what the hell he was going to do about Natalya Vasin.

***

Reed lifted the weights and did another punishing set of reps. His biceps were burning, his lungs heaving. Finally he set them down.

He paused to see if he'd purged the chaotic emotions inside him. His brain instantly went to the memories of holding Natalya up to that vent, her body pressed against his. Then that kiss. God, she'd tasted so fucking good. He'd wanted to lift her up, slam her against the wall and shove the last few inches of that damn skirt up so he could get to her.

Nope, he needed to lift a lot more weights. He started another set.

Dammit, he was trying to do what was best for her. She needed time, to heal, to regain her footing. The last thing she needed was him barreling in and taking her over. Because he would. He had been holding back because if he unleashed everything he had inside for her, she'd run screaming.

He never wanted Natalya to be afraid of him.

He remembered Jo. She'd been his goddamn hero. The best SEAL he'd ever worked with. She'd been a few years older than him and happy to mentor the new recruit. When she'd been taken captive in Central Africa, he'd been the first to volunteer to rescue her. She'd survived, endured terrible things, but they'd brought her home.

And she'd never been the same. Then she'd rushed into a relationship that had ended her.

"MacKinnon?"

He glanced across the gym. Shaw was waving at him.

"Come spar with us," the sniper said. "Looks like you need it."

Reed set the weights back in the rack. He eyed

44

Shaw and Claudia, who were squaring off with Gabe. Gabe was a machine in a fight. Reed didn't know the full story, but apparently he'd been in some secret Army program and was stronger and faster than normal. It was always two or three of them against Gabe when they sparred.

"Sure." Maybe fighting off this obsession he had with a woman who needed his care but refused it was just what he needed.

He moved out onto the mat. Shaw was ripping off his sweat-soaked T-shirt. The sniper was a little leaner than Reed and a lot leaner than Gabe, but he was all muscle and Reed knew from previous sparring sessions that he was fast.

Claudia was watching Shaw, an unreadable look on her face. Her gaze flicked to Reed and she smiled and clapped her hands together. "Ready? I think the three of us can take the big guy down." She faced Gabe who stood there, relaxed, arms by his sides. "Besides, his brains are all addled by love." She said the word like it was a fatal infectious disease. "So he'll be easier to flatten."

"You got something against love, Frost?" Shaw asked.

Claudia rolled her head to the side, stretching her neck, and jumped on the spot, her toned muscles flexing. "Don't need love to have some fun." She arched a brow. "I thought you already knew this, Mr. King of the Quickies."

He scowled. "I don't always have quickies, Frost. Sometimes I like to take my time, and go nice and slow." Then his scowl deepened. "Who the hell have you been having fun with? I thought you froze most guys out if they got within striking distance."

She shrugged. "None of your business. Now, can we whip Gabe's butt?"

The three of them fanned out in front of Gabe. The big man, with his impassive face, seemed supremely unconcerned at facing three of them.

Shaw went in first.

He got some good hits in, moving fast and dodging Gabe's blows. But it wasn't long before Shaw faceplanted into the mats.

Claudia rushed in with a powerful front kick. She and Gabe traded blows, and she was surprisingly graceful for such a strong, tough woman.

Shaw bounced back up. "Come on, let's take him down."

Reed nodded and together they waded in.

It felt good. The camaraderie of his squadmates, the physicality of the fight, the release of sweating out his frustration. As Gabe's fist hit his jaw, Reed winced and spun. He saw Shaw and Claudia working together. Shaw gave her a boost and her roundhouse kick hit Gabe squarely in the face.

The man barely reacted. He grabbed Claudia's leg, yanked, caught her in his arms then tossed her toward Shaw.

The two of them went down in a tangle of arms and legs, their joint curses filling the air.

Reed circled Gabe slowly. Damn, the man was beyond good. Reed struck out with his fists, feinted and ducked. Gabe moved, and as he swung out,

Reed gripped the man's arm and pulled back.

Reed dropped his weight, and as his back hit the mat, Gabe sailed over his head. Now it was a race to see who could get up first.

But before Reed could get his feet under him, Gabe was up, putting one foot in the center of Reed's chest. He exerted enough pressure to make Reed hiss.

"Got me." Reed held his hands up.

"Not a bad move," Gabe conceded.

"Get off me, you oaf." Claudia's snarky voice.

"Your ponytail is caught on my belt buckle. Quit twisting and hold on a sec."

Reed and Gabe glanced over. The other two were still flat on the mat. Claudia's dark hair was tangled in Shaw's belt, her face dangerously close to the sniper's crotch. He was trying to untangle her, but she was jerking around like a wildcat caught on a leash.

Reed grinned. Even Gabe's lips twitched.

"Want a beer?" Reed asked.

"Yeah," Gabe said.

They headed to the small mini-fridge in the corner. After popping the tops off a couple of homebrews, they leaned against the wall and continued to watch the show of Claudia and Shaw still snarling at each other.

"Any news? Did Marcus say any more on the hybrid?" Reed asked.

Gabe shrugged. "I spoke with Emerson. Her team checked them all over, but she doesn't think our scans pick up the hybrid DNA if the transformation to raptor is in the early stages."

"Damn. That mean we have to start quarantining all new arrivals?"

"Maybe."

Reed frowned. That was the last thing traumatized people needed. To be locked up like animals. And his thoughts turned to the problem of how Natalya had tracked the hybrid. How had she known the creature was in the comp lab?

"I reckon the raptors will start trying to hit the base more," Gabe said in a quiet voice.

"What?" Reed looked over at the other man.

"Before we were just a menace, hitting at patrols here and there. Blowing up small facilities. But when we took out the Genesis Facility…"

Yeah. It was a big, important target. Reed thought of that huge amber dome filled with hundreds of special genesis tanks being used to turn humans into aliens. It had taken time for the aliens to set that up, and Reed himself had pressed the detonator to blow it sky-high. "Now we're on their radar. They'll start trying to hit us more."

Plus, there was a large group of humans here they could put in those tanks. It was the reason the aliens had come to Earth. The resources and human tech were just bonuses…it was human bodies the aliens wanted most.

"Cruz said Santha's team has noted a lot of movement around the aliens' ship," Gabe continued.

Santha headed up a team of intel officers who crept into raptor territory and crept out again. The remote-operated drones could feed back a lot of information, but Santha's team was bringing back on-the-ground info worth its weight in rations.

Reed had seen the aliens' huge spaceship resting near the remnants of Sydney's airport. The gigantic thing looked like a beast that should be swimming through some prehistoric ocean. "You think they might be getting ready to leave?"

Gabe's gray eyes leveled on Reed.

Reed took another swig of beer. "I know. Wishful thinking."

"Damn it, give me some of that." Claudia strode up and snatched Reed's beer. She downed what was left. "What are you guys talking about?"

"Raptors, what else?" Reed answered.

Her face hardened. "I wish there was something more we could do to them. I'm sick of just nipping at their heels."

Reed agreed. They'd been hoping to slowly wear the aliens down. But deep inside, he knew they needed something bigger. They had to be more than just a pest for the raptors to kick about with their boots.

Or they'd never be free.

"So, Reed," Shaw said about as casually as an autocannon to the face, "heard you got locked up with the pretty Dr. Vasin."

Reed tensed a little. "Yeah."

"All alone in a storage room. By yourselves."

Claudia rolled her eyes and opened the mini-fridge. She pulled out a beer and tossed it to Reed.

Then she tossed another one to Shaw, which almost hit the man's head.

"Hey." He snatched it out of the air before it made contact and popped the top. "I was just saying. She's filled out nicely, and those glasses, and the sexy little skirts she wears..." He made a humming noise.

Reed's hand tightened on his bottle, his knuckles turning white. "Baird."

Shaw's eyes widened theatrically, and he grinned. "Oh, sorry. Nice lady. Smart, nice, very nice."

Claudia opened her own beer. "Well, any truth to Shaw's subtle-as-a-sledgehammer questioning?"

Reed shrugged. "She's been through a lot."

"She's a tough woman," Gabe said. "We all saw what she survived."

"I know. So she needs more time to recover from that."

Claudia ran her tongue over her teeth. "You decide that for her? Or is the alpha-male soldier pounding his chest?"

Reed looked at her and stayed silent.

Claudia nodded and sipped her beer. "Men are idiots."

He bristled. "I only want what's best for her. I'm putting my needs second to hers."

"No you're not. You feel all protective and shit, and those are your needs. You're taking her choices away, and you know what? The raptors, they already did that."

God, the bottom dropped out of Reed's stomach.

Was that how Natalya saw it? He raked a hand through his hair. *Dammit all to hell.*

Chapter Five

After several hours of tossing and turning in her bed, Natalya decided to just get up and do some work. The energy cubes were calling to her, anyway.

She clicked on a light. Her quarters weren't big. Just a single room with a narrow bunk, a tiny kitchenette, and living area with an adjoining bathroom. At first, she'd hated the quarters. They were too small, and the lack of windows made her feel like she was in a box. But the huge painting on the wall helped.

It was all bright colors—strokes, splatters and dollops of paint. Orange, yellow, red, blue and green. One of her fellow lab survivors, a young girl named Bryony, had painted it for her.

Looking at it now made Natalya smile. Bryony was still healing, but the resilient young thing had shaken off the horrors of what had been done to her. In the painting, Natalya saw simple joy, happiness and hope.

Bryony had been adopted by Cruz Ramos and his partner, Santha. The ten-year-old was excited and busy getting ready to be a big sister to the baby Santha was expecting. The fact that it wouldn't be born for another eight months didn't bother Bryony.

The girl was Natalya's secret hero. She really, really wished she could shake off what had happened to them as easily as the little girl had. But it just wasn't that easy. Regardless, Natalya would keep trying to follow Bryony's example. Latch onto life and find happiness where she could.

Which, of course, made her think of Reed.

She wanted him. She took a deep breath. She wanted sex, and laughter, and someone to hold her tight. Someone to help make her forget, and make her hope for more. She rubbed her hand against her forehead. But she couldn't be with him if she knew he wasn't giving her his entire self.

Maybe she'd have to think about what she could do to make him see *her*. See past the victim.

Natalya turned to her living area, which was dominated by a desk she'd had moved in and her comp sitting on top of it.

And resting beside the comp were the two energy cubes.

For now, she had these to focus on. She stared at the blinking light on the live one. At least her work didn't twist her up inside. It was one thing that soothed her and made her feel in control.

She sat in her chair and picked up the cubes. *Time to tell me your secrets.* She lost track of time as she worked. She measured energy output, ran scans. Both cubes seemed almost identical, with faint grooves she guessed were decorative as she couldn't see any other obvious reason for them. She lifted the cube that wasn't operational. She couldn't see a reason why it wouldn't work.

Unless she pulled it apart.

She sank back in her chair, tugging the hem of her white, button-down sleepshirt. She didn't like thinking that it had probably belonged to some now-dead businessman.

A movement at the corner of her room caught her eye. She gasped, jumping to her feet. Her chair fell over and clattered to the floor.

Heart beating, she lifted a closed fist to her chest. There was nothing there. Just shadows. Just nightmares trying to haunt her. It was always worst in the middle of the night, all alone, with only the past for company.

She tried some deep breathing. She'd visited the base therapist once and the woman had taught her a few methods for easing panic attacks. But Natalya hadn't been back. Talking about the past, about the lab, just made her feel worse, not better.

She wanted to be bold, be confident again. She didn't want to be a mouse to be coaxed or looked after. She wanted to charge up to Reed MacKinnon and kiss him, yank his shirt off and lick those hard abs of his. She wanted to see how long and thick his cock was, taste it, feel it inside her.

God. She went damp between her legs. She rubbed her thighs together to try and ease the ache. She desperately wanted to know how she and Reed would fit together.

Her gaze fell on the cubes again. And on the grooves etched on the edges of them. *Fit together.*

Fit together.

She hurried back to her desk, excitement surging. She lifted the cubes, studying the faint grooves. She and Noah hadn't given them much attention because they hadn't seemed important.

Natalya lifted the cubes, turning them, lining up the grooves.

The cubes clicked together.

And the non-operational cube flared to life, red lights flashing, while the lights on the other cube turned brighter and pulsed a golden-orange.

Her eyes widened. She snatched up her analyzer and ran it over them. The energy output was higher. She reached for her comp, tapping notes into it. It made sense now. The newer cube was a command cube. It carried the instructions and controls. She turned the joined cubes over. There were more grooves.

Ingenious. You could clip multiple cubes together, increasing the power source as required. A couple of cubes could maybe power a vehicle. An armload, maybe a ptero ship. She chewed on her lip. A whole stack of them a facility—she swallowed—like a lab.

Or even a huge alien spaceship.

She touched the command cube. Could she hack into it? Could she do something to it that would render it useless?

It pulsed again and she felt an electric shock through her body. *Ow.* She snatched her hand back and the cubes clattered onto her desk. Tingles raced through her, and they weren't the pleasant kind.

The sensation seemed to settle in her chest. Her heart jerked and started a rapid, painful rhythm. Gasping, she clutched her chest, and lurched to her feet.

She tried to pull in air, but panic was seizing her. She couldn't breathe.

Couldn't. Breathe.

She stumbled toward her door. Help. She needed help. Somehow, she got out of her room. She staggered down the empty tunnel, slamming into the wall a few times.

She wasn't really thinking; she just kept trying to get air into her burning lungs and moving her feet. Her skin felt hot, and damp with perspiration. Her heart felt like it was going to burst out of her chest.

She reached a door and slammed her palms against it, sobbing. She slid down until her knees hit the concrete.

The door opened. Reed stood there, bare-chested, jeans unsnapped, tawny hair tousled.

"Shit." He crouched and scooped her into his arms. "I've got you, brown-eyed girl. I've got you."

She leaned into him. With his arms around her, she believed everything would be all right. But the pain in her chest made her moan.

***

Reed strode down the tunnel, jaw tight, and his

arms secure around a shaking Natalya.

The way she was shivering, and curled in on herself...he was damned worried.

As soon as she saw the infirmary door appear ahead, she started struggling. "No."

"Something's wrong. You need to get checked out."

"*No*. No more tests, no more prodding. I'm fine." She jerked again and he had to tighten his hold not to drop her. She was fighting like a wild woman.

"Something's wrong. You're seeing the doc."

"The energy cubes. I was working with them and I got some kind of shock."

He frowned. "Then you definitely need to get checked out."

"Please." This time her voice was a harsh whisper, her brown eyes so large he could drown in them. "Please, Reed."

Shit. He breathed in, evaluating his options. Finally, he grabbed his communicator from his pocket and dialed up a name.

"Hello?" A sleepy female voice.

"Emerson? Reed. Something's wrong with Natalya. She got some kind of energy shock from the alien tech she was working on. She's not well."

There was the rumble of a male voice in the background. Gabe.

Reed continued. "She won't go to the infirmary. Could you meet me at my quarters?"

"Sure thing." The doctor sounded more awake now. "Five minutes."

Reed headed back the way he'd come. Natalya

was still shaking, but she'd settled down.

"I don't want to be checked out," she said, tone mutinous.

"Too bad. Infirmary or Emerson. Your choice."

Natalya muttered under her breath. "Not really a choice."

"It is. I know you want to control your life again, but I won't compromise your health."

She was silent for the rest of the trip. He pressed his palm to his door lock and carried her inside.

He flicked on the lights and winced. Damn, he should have tidied up a bit. His bed was unmade, and there were clothes tossed over his couch. Dust was gathering in his postage-stamp-sized kitchen because he never, ever used it. And the center of the room was dominated by the makings of a mountain bike he was working on. He scavenged parts for it, and when he had free time, he was putting it together. He had no idea if he'd ever get to ride it, but he hoped so. One day.

He set Natalya on the couch. Hurriedly, he scooped up his clothes, opened the bathroom door and tossed them inside.

She was still shaking, her arms wrapped around herself, but she was looking around. "You're messy."

He cleared his throat. "Ah, yeah. Keeping things tidy is not my strong suit."

Large brown eyes met his. "I'm very tidy."

He smiled. "Yeah, I'd guessed as much." And boy, did he want to mess her up a little.

It was then he realized she was wearing...not very much. That man's shirt left her legs very, very bare. All that smooth skin... *Damn. She's hurt, MacKinnon. Get a grip.*

Suddenly, he was irrationally jealous of the shirt. Lying on her skin, against places he wanted to see, caress, kiss. He huffed out a breath. And he really hated that it was some other man's shirt. He knew she would have gotten it at the base clothing store, and had no idea who it had once belonged to, but he had the urge to see her in one of his T-shirts. Soft cotton draped over her high, firm breasts.

The door chimed.

He let Emerson and Gabe in. The big man gave him a nod and they stood together as Emerson hurried over to Natalya, carrying a small medical bag.

"What happened?" There was a frown on Doc Emerson's face as she studied the other woman.

Natalya explained what had transpired with the cubes. "I'm really feeling better now. I think I might have just had a panic attack, that's all."

"I'm going to run a scan." Emerson lifted her m-scanner.

Natalya tensed and Reed moved closer, pressing a hand to her shoulder.

"Nothing intrusive, Natalya, I promise." Emerson somehow kept her voice no-nonsense and soothing. "Just let me make sure you're okay."

Reed squeezed Natalya's shoulder and finally, she gave a short nod.

She did seem better. Her skin wasn't pale and clammy anymore. And her shaking had stopped.

A few seconds later, Emerson clicked off the scanner. "Everything seems okay. Your heartrate is a little elevated, but I'd say it'll calm down."

Natalya nodded.

"I suggest some sleep, not work."

Gabe made a sound in his throat and Reed raised an eyebrow.

"Funny to hear her give that advice to someone," Gabe said, voice low.

Emerson pulled a face. "Can it, big guy. I'm getting better at it."

Again, Natalya curled her arms around herself. "I've...been having trouble sleeping."

"I can give you something to help—"

"No." Natalya shook her head vehemently. "No, no drugs."

Damn the fucking raptors. Reed wanted to tear them apart for what they'd done to her.

"Okay," Emerson conceded with a sigh. "Then I recommend you find something to help you relax. I'd suggest a hot shower or a bubble bath, but I know the water's cold this time of night and you don't have a tub. Maybe some warm milk? Some gentle music?"

"I'll make sure she sleeps," Reed said.

The doctor's mouth twitched. "I'm sure you will." She picked her small medical bag up and eyed Reed again. "Sex is also a good relaxant."

Natalya made a choked noise. Reed smiled and shook his head. "We'll take that under advisement, Doc."

"All right, my job here is done." Emerson straightened and turned to Gabe. "Come on, big guy. Now I'm awake, I might need something to help me relax."

Gabe smiled. "A bubble bath?"

Emerson strode out the door and glanced over her shoulder. "No. That's definitely not what I had in mind."

Gabe nodded at Reed and hurried out after his woman.

When Reed looked over, Natalya had folded her legs up to her chest, her cheek pressed to one knee. She looked as though the tiniest thing would make her shatter. But if he told her that, she'd probably give him a tongue lashing. He knew she had a core of strength in there, but right now she needed a lifeline.

An idea sparked. He held out a hand. "Come on."

"Where are we going?"

He swung her back into his arms. "To do something I know will help you relax."

Chapter Six

When Reed carried her out of the tunnel and into the crisp night, Natalya breathed in a huge lungful of air.

Spring had arrived, and while the air was cool, it wasn't cold. Actually, it felt good on her skin. Refreshing. Cleansing.

He carried her through the trees, following a path he clearly knew well. She knew he snuck out of the base whenever the need struck him. He had outdoorsman stamped all over him, so living underground had to be difficult for him.

"I can walk," she said.

He shook his head. "Nope. I like carrying you."

And she liked being carried. She wasn't big but she wasn't small, either, yet he carried her with an ease that made the feminine part of her sigh.

She knew where they were headed, but when he finally stopped and set her on her feet she still felt the beauty of the scenery wash over her. Moonlight glinted on the swimming hole. It wasn't large, but it was pretty. It was roughly a circle and surrounded by large boulders and rocks. The dense bush came right to the ring of rocks at the water's edge and there was just something so...calming and tranquil about it.

"Going in?" he asked.

She caught her lip between her teeth. She was desperate to feel the cool water on her skin. Should she go in with her shirt on? Make him turn around? Or finally reclaim a small part of her confidence?

She nodded, then started unbuttoning her shirt.

Reed straightened like he'd been hit with a stun gun. His gaze zeroed in on her hands. She took her time, slipping each button out.

When they were all undone, she clasped the sides of the shirt, ready to slide it off. She hesitated. Her scar was...ugly. She could have gotten rid of it, but she just didn't want to undergo any more medical procedures.

Well, it was a part of her now, for better or worse. She shrugged her shoulders and let the shirt fall to her feet.

Reed's hot gaze slid over her, lingering on her breasts, her belly and the juncture of her thighs. Oh, it felt so good to have a man look at her like that. To have *this* man look at her like that.

In the moonlight, she could easily make out the bulge at the front of his pants. The sight caused her breath to hitch. Then, she forced her gaze away, turned, and did a shallow dive into the pool.

The water was very cool, bordering on cold. But it invigorated her.

Okay, maybe the fact that she was naked in front of Reed had a little bit to do with it, too.

She surfaced and turned.

The rocky bank of the waterhole was empty.

Frowning, she treaded water, looking around. There was a ripple on the surface of the water, like someone else had dived in.

She waited for him to surface.

And waited.

Her pulse tripped. He'd been under a long time. She turned in circles, searching the smooth surface for any sign of him.

A hand gripped her ankle and gently tugged. She yelped and Reed pushed out of the water right in front of her, water streaming off him.

"You were under so long." Natalya knew her voice sounded just a little breathless. All those muscles. His shoulders and chest were so hard, so sculpted.

"Navy SEAL, sweetheart. We like the water. I can hold my breath a very long time." He slicked his now-wet hair back. The look accented the rugged lines of his face.

For the first time, she noticed the tension lines bracketing his mouth. He was tired. And worried. She always thought of him as a rock, solid as stone. But every day he went out there and risked his life fighting the raptors.

She'd seen him during her rescue. Had worried when he and the rest of Hell Squad had been in a Hawk crash. And tonight, he'd faced down a raptor to protect her, not to mention been worried about her.

Reed deserved some relaxation too.

"Well then, a badass Navy SEAL like yourself

should be able to catch me." She spun and dived into the water.

Natalya had always liked swimming. After all, she'd grown up in Australia, where swimming was a favorite pastime for most kids. She dived down, kicking as fast as she could.

When she came up for air, she spotted Reed powering through the water toward her. She squeaked and lunged to the left. Paddling with everything she had, she reached the rocky side and clung to it, her gaze darting around the pool. She didn't see him.

She searched the dark water, but there was no sign. Then, he surfaced a meter away from her, making her yelp. He lunged for her and she pushed off the rocks, laughing as she did.

They played a little longer, like kids, splashing each other, dodging outstretched arms. A few times, his hands slid along her legs. He made mock growling noises that sent her into fits of laughter.

Finally, with a powerful kick that launched him toward her, he grabbed her around the waist, lifting her up. She was still laughing. God, this felt so good. She felt light and free.

"Got you," he said.

His voice was deep and raspy, and as her gaze fell on his face, her laughter died away.

And another feeling rushed into her.

Desire. Strong and fierce.

She sank her hands into his hair and watched his eyes darken. Right at this moment, she felt powerful, vital, and she wanted to hold on to that.

"I want to kiss you, but this time you do it properly," she said.

"Natalya—"

She tugged his hair, hard. "No holding back."

"Just a kiss," he growled.

We'll see. She leaned forward and nipped at his bottom lip.

He growled again and it sent goose bumps over her skin. Then he slanted his mouth over hers and kissed her.

This. This was how Reed MacKinnon kissed. This was his desire unleashed...and it was as scorching as a backfire explosive. As the force of his need hit her, his mouth pulling on hers, his tongue delving against hers, she realized this was exactly what she wanted. What she needed.

She kissed him back, pulling him closer. A small moan came from her throat.

Reed's arms tightened, mashing her bare breasts against his chest. *Oh.* She wrapped her legs around his lean waist.

And felt the hard brush of his cock against her thigh.

He pulled back, panting. His hands pushed her away gently until there was some water between them.

"Why did you stop?" she demanded breathlessly.

"Only a kiss. No more."

Irritation flashed through her. "I want you. I want to touch you, feel you inside me."

He cursed and with a few strong kicks, dragged her to the side. He pushed out of the pool with one arm, muscles flexing. Then he was yanking his jeans over a mighty fine ass.

"You aren't making this easy for me."

She gripped the edge, her fingers digging into rock. "I'm making it very easy for you. I want you, you want me."

He turned, shoving his hands on his hips. "An hour ago you were shaking, hurt and in pain. I am *not* going to take advantage of you."

Something hard and angry inside Natalya eased. It wasn't that he didn't want her. Her gaze dropped to the straining denim before going back to his face. He was just being Reed. Heroic and noble.

"Even if I really want this? And you do, too?"

"I won't rush this," he said, his tone firm. "I told you about my friend. Her name was Jo. She'd been held captive for six damn months. They'd tortured her, raped her, kept her in a cage, but she survived." He shoved a hand through his hair. "Then she rushed into a relationship with another soldier. He...took her over. He wore down the last of her confidence, stifled her, until finally there was nothing of Jo left."

Natalya felt the pulse of his grief, her fingers pressing hard into the rock. "What happened to her?"

"She committed suicide."

God. Natalya climbed out of the pool and stood in front of him. She didn't care that she was naked and dripping wet. "Reed, I'm sorry about Jo—"

"When we do this—and make no mistake, we will—you'll be one hundred percent ready for everything I have to give you. Got it?"

His gaze was hot and burning. It turned her insides molten and her knees weak. "I'm not your friend."

"We need to get back," he muttered.

She stamped a foot. "You aren't listening to me—"

He snatched up her shirt and tossed it to her. "You can have a hissy fit, but I won't change my mind. I'm looking out for you whether you like it or not. That's the man I am, I can't be any different."

She yanked her shirt on. It stuck to her damp skin. "Fine. Maybe I'll find someone who will listen to me. Someone who wants me enough to accept what I'm offering."

His eyes narrowed and he yanked her close, his face an inch from hers. "Don't push me, Natalya."

She pulled back and started doing up her buttons. Anger was a nasty taste in her mouth. God, she was a mess. She wasn't even sure why she was angry at him. He was just taking care of her. All she knew was that she was a hot ball of need and the man she wanted was pushing her away.

"Fine, Reed. You win. You don't want me enough, I get it." She spun, intent on hiding the tiny knot of hurt inside and stomping back to base.

Then Reed muttered something and grabbed the hem of her shirt. He yanked her back and spun her to face him.

His features were carved like granite. "You want to see how much I want you?" He slashed his hand down, tearing her shirt open.

She gasped, her belly clenching.

***

A voice in Reed's head kept telling him to back off.

But the mere idea of Natalya in another man's arms had gripped him, shoving him over the edge.

He pulled her close and kissed her, the force of it bending her head back. Her hands clutched at his bare shoulders, her nails scoring his skin.

God, she tasted good. And those damn little noises she made in her throat almost did him in. But somehow, somewhere, he dredged up a thin thread of control. He pulled back.

"No," she moaned in frustration.

"Shh." He lifted her and lay her back on a thick patch of grass.

She lay there looking up at him, her skin pale under the moonlight. With her short elfin hair and sensuous curves, she could truly be an elf, come to steal the heart of a simple, mortal man.

He circled her waist with his hands. They looked large and brutish compared to her elegant softness. He skimmed his hands up, framing her ribs. Even in the shadows, he saw her scar. He reached out and traced a finger up it.

She flinched and gripped his wrist. "Reed, no. It's ugly."

"It's a badge of courage." He leaned down and put his lips to it. Tracing it with his tongue. "A badge of survival."

She moaned again, arching up to his mouth.

He reached her breasts and moved to the left, sucking one taut nipple into his mouth. Her moans turned to little cries. Oh, yeah, his brown-eyed girl liked that. Soon he switched to the other and gave it the same attention. She moved restlessly under him, igniting a dark need that he had to ruthlessly keep in check.

This was about her.

Now he reversed his path, dragging his mouth over her smooth belly. He nipped her hipbone, his hands digging into her hips.

"Reed." She wrapped one long leg around his waist. It pushed the warm, damp heart of her against his hard cock.

Fuck. He gripped her thigh and pulled her leg off him.

Confusion flashed in her eyes. "No," she cried. "You can't—"

"I'm not going to fuck you, Natalya. Not tonight." Her face fell.

"Hey." He framed her cheeks. "One day I will. I'll fuck you so hard, you'll feel me for days. I'll take my time and worship every part of you. But tonight, you had a bad moment. You were shaking in my arms and I was frightened as hell. Tonight, just let me make you feel good." He took her hands in his and pressed her arms above her head. "You keep them there or I'll stop."

Her eyes flashed. "I can't touch you?"

"Nope." He nipped her belly, enjoyed the choked sound that came from her throat.

"That's not fair." Defiantly, she reached a hand

out to his shoulder.

Reed pulled away from her.

"No!" She moved her arm, letting her hand fall back against the soft grass above her head. But she moved restlessly, clearly not happy with the situation.

"There's my good girl."

"You're a torturer. I should have known that annoying patience of yours tended to...other things."

He smiled and moved his lips lower, lower. He trailed one hand up her thigh, pushing her legs apart. "I promise you'll enjoy it. All you have to do is lie back and feel."

He parted the dark curls between her legs, then lowered his head. At the touch of his tongue, she cried out. He licked her, delving into her, exploring her sweet folds. Damn, she tasted so good.

Reed heard every little cry, felt every jerk. He licked her, nuzzled her, caught her swollen clit between his teeth, then sucked.

"Oh...Reed. Don't stop."

But he did ease back slightly, before sliding one finger up, circling her, and thrusting it inside her. Her hips moved in rhythm with his thrusts. He slid a second finger in and she moaned. Damn, she was tight. She'd feel so good around his cock.

He licked his lips, tasted her honey and wanted more. Pulling his fingers out, he slid his hands under the rounded cheeks of her ass and lifted her up to his mouth. Once more, he tasted her, working her hard with his mouth and tongue.

Her hands slapped down beside her, fingers twisting in the grass. He felt her orgasm coming, felt the sweet tension growing in her body.

With another lick of her clit, she exploded and screamed his name.

He moved so his head was pressed against her belly and he stroked her skin as she came down.

Finally, he looked up at her. She was watching him with lazy, sated eyes. She looked the most relaxed he'd ever seen her and that made him pretty damn happy.

"I want you," she said baldly.

Her simple honesty cut through him, making his cock throb. "I want you too, brown-eyed girl." His words were a growl. He pushed up, covering her body with his, and claimed her mouth.

Soon they were straining against each other, rolling over the grass. She clamped her arms and legs around him. Damn, he couldn't hold back any longer. He had to have her, mark her, make her his. To hell with waiting. She wanted him so badly her desire left him singed.

A sharp beeping cut through the red haze of desire. His communicator.

"Dammit." He sat up, yanking the device from his pocket.

"No," she moaned.

"I know." The timing sucked. He glanced at the screen and cursed. "Hell Squad's getting called out. We have to get back to base."

She closed her eyes, then opened them and nodded.

HELL SQUAD: REED

He cupped her cheek. "Later. We'll finish this."

She licked her lips. "Later."

His cock throbbed. "Witch. Come on." He pulled her close to him.

Together, they fastened her shirt as best they could. Damn. He had to get her back to her room before anyone saw her like this.

"You owe me a shirt," she grumbled.

He grabbed her hand and led her into the trees. "You bet. I look forward to seeing you lying back on my bunk, wearing my shirt, with my come drying on your thighs."

Her lips parted. "Stop that. God, you drive me crazy."

"I have another fantasy." He lowered his voice. "I want to fuck you on your desk in the comp lab while you're wearing one of those tight skirts of yours rucked up around your hips."

"Reed!" Her breathing sped up a little. "Hopefully not while Noah or any of the others on the tech team are around."

"Hell, no! No one sees you naked but me. Got it?"

She smiled, her teeth white in the darkness. "Got it."

Chapter Seven

Reed leapt off the Hawk. He was hot, sweaty and tired. The rest of Hell Squad exited behind him. The landing pads were busy as always, and a small crew rushed over to check the Hawk.

At least he wasn't covered in raptor blood...for a change. Their mission had turned into simple recon.

A fucking large troop of raptor soldiers was setting up a base in the remnants of a nearby town. Too bloody close to Blue Mountain Base for any of them to be happy.

Hell Squad had hidden and taken a buttload of photos of the raptors bringing in supplies. He swung his mayhem over his shoulder. Now they had to decide what to do about it.

"Need to brief Holmes," Marcus said.

The rest of the squad nodded. Then Reed spotted Natalya hurrying toward him. She was dressed in a dark-gray skirt that shaped over her curves, with a pale-blue shirt tucked into it, emphasizing her waist and hourglass figure.

Damn. Even being as hot and tired as he was, his cock responded.

"Hi." She lifted a hand and waved.

"Natalya," Marcus said as the rest of the squad grunted and waved.

She shot Reed a small, private smile he felt all the way to his bones. Then she looked at Marcus again. "I've been waiting for you to come back." She took in a deep breath. "I think I've worked out a way to use the energy cubes against the raptors."

Marcus' blue gaze caught Reed's over Natalya's head. "Go on."

"The energy cube Reed brought in...it's a command cube. It can be added to others and it controls them. I've also discovered we have to be really careful with them...I only got a small electric shock but they are capable of killing if used incorrectly."

Shit. A muscle ticked in Reed's jaw. She could have killed herself when that cube had shocked her.

"But that's not what I wanted to tell you." A hesitant smile. "I've worked out a way to upload a virus to it that would essentially kill any other cubes it's attached to. It renders them useless."

"The raptors couldn't get energy from them, then?" Reed asked.

She shook her head. "And I think it would destroy some key components in the cubes."

"Meaning?" Marcus prompted.

"Meaning they wouldn't be able to repair the cubes and use them again. Ever."

"Damn," Shaw said. "That is sweet, Natalya. Good work."

Reed grabbed her and yanked her off her feet.

He pressed a quick kiss to her lips. "Nice work, brown-eyed girl."

Heat colored her cheeks and she shot a quick sideways glance at Hell Squad. All of whom were grinning at them. "Ah...thanks."

"All right. Showers will have to wait," Marcus rasped. "Everyone to Ops. I'll have the general meet us there."

"Come on." Reed pulled Natalya along with him.

Soon they pushed through the doors to the Operations Area. Inside, the large room nicknamed the Hive, was busy with rows of drone operators sitting in front of live-feed screens. Other people bustled around carrying tablets.

Hell Squad moved to a conference room off the main room. Someone had taped a sign to the door that said "Hell Squad." They'd also drawn a caricature of a muscle-bound, gun-wielding soldier stomping on a raptor. Reed thought it was pretty good.

In the room, he pulled out a chair for Natalya at the large conference table. As she sat and crossed her legs, her skirt hem lifted and he stared at her legs. God, he had to have her soon.

He looked up and noticed Shaw grinning at him. Reed shook his head at the sniper, then took up a position against the wall with the rest of the squad. They were all too dirty to sit in the chairs. A minute later, General Holmes strode in, followed by Elle.

"Hell Squad." He nodded at them. Holmes, in his neat and tidy uniform, carried an air of command.

He'd been a poster boy for the Army—a young, handsome and talented general who'd shot up through the ranks. He often rankled the troops, but no one could fault his dedication.

Reed thought the man looked tired. Since the first hybrid had snuck into the base, Holmes had been busy devising ways to keep the raptors from infiltrating again. And reassuring the spooked residents. The second hybrid would have made his job that much more difficult.

Holmes yanked a chair out and sat. He raked a hand through his dark hair with its dash of silver at the temples. "What have you got for me?"

Marcus clicked the comp controller and images of the raptors making their new base filled the screen. "This is a small town sixty kilometers south of Blue Mountain Base."

The general's jaw tightened. "You think they're planning an attack?"

"They don't appear to be, at least not in the immediate future," Marcus said. "But the location of this base indicates it must be on their agenda. They're flying in on pteros and, as always, are steering clear of the trees."

"Geek squad worked out why the raptors hate the trees?" Shaw asked.

Holmes shook his head. "All we have are theories. Maybe something to do with their vision, maybe some substance the trees give off that they don't like. Who knows, maybe they have killer trees on their planet."

Reed pondered the theories. The canids—the

raptors' alien-hunting dogs—hated cedar oil. Now all the squads carried cedar oil grenades. It was possible there was something else in the trees that acted as some sort of repellent.

"So we think they're getting ready to hit our base?" Reed said. "Payback for the Genesis Facility?"

"Yeah," Marcus agreed. "I'd guess we graduated from pains in the ass to viable threat."

The images were on slideshow, showing the raptors moving supplies into a building that must have once been a city hall. The next image showed a raptor ptero landing on the town's main street.

"Stop!" Natalya leapt to her feet. "Stop on that image."

Reed narrowed his gaze, staring at the boxes the raptors were moving into the building. "What is it? They're just boxes."

She pointed. "No, they aren't. Go back one image."

Marcus clicked back. And this time, because Reed was staring at the boxes, he saw what he'd missed the first time. Some of the boxes were blinking with red lights.

"Those are energy cubes joined together." She swiveled, beaming at him. "That's the power source for whatever they're doing at this new location."

Shit. And Natalya had a way to neutralize the cubes. They could take out the raptor's power source at this new base. And at their other facilities.

"And?" General Holmes asked, frowning.

"I've found a way to upload a virus to one of the command cubes. We click it into those—" she pointed again "—and it'll destroy their energy supply."

"Hot damn," Claudia said.

"So, you get this cube ready and show us what to do," Reed said. "And we can head out and finish this alien base."

Natalya shook her head. "It's too complicated. None of you have the capability to do it."

"She just call us dumb?" Shaw asked.

Natalya straightened, all prim and proper. "Of course not. But could you tell me how to use a carbine right now and then send me out to kill raptors? I need to be the one to set the cube in place and run my virus program on the spot."

"No." The word burst out of Reed. "I won't let you do this."

She slowly came to her feet. "It's not your choice. It's mine."

"It's too dangerous. Look at all those raptors, Natalya. You want to end up back in their hands?"

She flinched and he hated himself. But he had to keep her safe.

"You are not getting close to those fuckers. Not while I'm still breathing."

"Reed," Marcus said, his voice weary.

"You know better than any of us that nothing good comes from taking untrained civilians on missions. Remember Elle and the rex?"

Marcus' face darkened and Elle shot a glare at Reed.

He looked at Gabe. "Emerson got taken by raptors."

Menace radiated off the big, silent man.

"Natalya's been through enough," Reed said.

A slim hand landed on his arm. He looked down into big brown eyes that caught his entire attention.

"I need to do this, Reed."

"No—"

Her fingers tightened on him. "Listen to me. I need to fight back. I want to strike at them, not just be a victim."

He grabbed her arms now. "You aren't a victim, you're a survivor."

A faint smile tweaked her lips. "Then let me be a survivor. This is my decision and I need to know you'll support me and have my back."

Dammit. He pulled away, scraping a hand through his hair. She was asking for him to go against every instinct he had. But he knew, deep down, that she needed this and she needed him to be with her every step of the way. He gave the conference table a solid kick and heard the crack of wood.

"All right, Natalya, you're in," Marcus said. "But we need twenty-four hours to recuperate and plan." Marcus' gaze landed on Reed. "You take that time and spend it with her showing her how to defend herself."

***

"This is a Xeon 5 laser pistol."

Natalya watched Reed pick up the small weapon from the vast array on the bench. And she heard the whip of anger simmering in his voice.

He was still mad at her.

He turned to face her. "It's one of the smallest and lightest of the laser pistols, so it'll be easy for you to handle." He held it out. "Some of its components are plastic. The tech guys have a 3-D printer, so we have several of these babies, as they're easy to make and maintain."

She took the pistol, testing the feel of it in her hands. It was light. She shot Reed a glance from under her lashes. His jaw was tight, tiny lines of strain were visible around his mouth, and he wasn't looking at her.

"Ear protection on." He nodded toward the earmuffs hanging on the wall. "Let's test it out."

They were at the base's shooting range. There were ten long rows, each with electronic targets at the end. There was only one other person using the range. The huge man with his dark hair in long dreadlocks had given them a nod when they'd entered. Since then, he'd been busy unloading a huge, booming weapon into the electronic targets that danced around like mad.

She pulled some earmuffs off the wall. "Who's that?" she asked.

"Tane. Tane Rahia. He's head of Squad Three."

The Berserkers. She stared at the man with wide eyes. She'd heard rumors about them. Tough, undisciplined, reckless.

Reed tapped her on the forehead. "Focus. We only have a few hours to get this done before you're going to head out right into the heart of a new raptor base and put yourself at risk."

Ouch. His tone was sharp as a knife's edge. "Reed, I know you're upset."

A muscle in his jaw flexed. "The pistol's simple. Aim and shoot. When the charge dies, take your finger off the trigger. It'll recharge in under two seconds."

With a sigh, she settled her muffs over her head and turned to face the target.

"Two hands." Reed's voice came through the muffs' speakers, as clear as without them. His arms also surrounded her, his big body pressing up behind hers.

Focus? How was she supposed to focus like this?

He helped her lift the pistol and aim it, her arms outstretched.

"Now, pull the trigger."

She did. Green laser fire whizzed down her lane. As it hit the electronic target, she saw it shimmer.

"It's got more kick than I'd guessed," she said.

He nodded, his chin brushing her head. "Again."

He made her shoot over and over again. Soon, her arms were burning from the strain. He gave her pointers, adjusted her grip, changed the targets to different sizes and distances.

And the entire time, he surrounded her, his body brushing against hers in a way she couldn't ignore. A hand along her arm, his chest against her back, his thighs against her bottom.

By the time he decided they were done, her body was a mass of quivering need. Every nerve ending was trembling and every cell was vitally aware of him.

His arms were still around her and he was saying...something about a holster and a gun safety.

Unable to stop herself, she pressed back against him, her butt brushing him.

He hissed out a breath. "Natalya."

She felt one very large and very hard cock nestle against the crevice of her bottom.

His arms tightened around her. "We have a mission, a dangerous one, to prepare for."

"I know. I'm—"

"Not taking it seriously enough." His words were like bullets past her ear. "If they get you, they'll put you back in a cage. Take you to a lab again...or kill you."

A rock settled on her chest. "I know—"

His fingers dug into her skin. "I can't bear the thought of them cutting into your soft skin again—" he dragged in a shaky breath "—of them crushing the life out of you."

"Stop it." She spun and slammed her hands against his chest. "You're trying to scare me."

His hands cupped her cheeks, lifting her gaze to his burning gold one. "Yeah, I am. I don't want you to go in there unprepared. You need the fear to give you an edge."

"I'll be with you. With Hell Squad."

"We aren't superheroes, Natalya. We all bleed too. Can be killed."

She did not want to think about Reed hurt or dying. It was hard enough knowing what he risked every time he went out there.

"This mission is important." She pressed her hands over his. "We'll do it, together, and strike back at them. They might not be the raptors who hurt me—" her voice wavered "—but I think it'll help to know I took the offensive."

He released a long breath and let his forehead drop to hers. "Okay. But I'll be by your side the entire time."

She smiled. "I'd like that."

"God, you twist me up."

She licked her lips. "Really? I don't think I've ever twisted a man up before." Especially not a hard, tough warrior like Reed. But boy, she liked it.

"If...if the worst happens—" he stopped with a curse and heaved in a breath. His gold eyes bored into hers. "If they get you, I'll come for you. Understand?"

She trembled. "Okay."

"You don't do anything stupid, or risk yourself, you wait until I come."

Natalya could barely stand the thought of being strapped down on a bed again, bright lights in her face, pain sawing through her. Panic fluttered in her chest. "Reed—"

He gave her a little shake. "Promise me, sweetheart, or I won't let you get on that Hawk."

Could she hold on if the aliens had her again?

Memories of being dragged away the first time flashed through her head. She wrapped her arms around him and pressed her face to his chest. Suddenly an overwhelming urge welled inside her, the need to talk.

"When they took me…I'd been hiding out at the university. That's where I was when the attack happened. A bunch of us, staff and students, had been there, scavenging, hiding. Then a raptor patrol came through."

Her throat tightened. She remembered the screams, the hiss of raptor poison burning through skin, wood and metal.

Reed's hand stroked down her back, steadying her. "My memories of the lab aren't always clear and my nightmares…sometimes I don't know what was real and what was imagined. But I had such little hope." She gripped him tighter and his arms held her tight and safe. She breathed him in, that salty-ocean scent of him. "There was so much pain, lights in my eyes, and sobbing. Mine, and the people around me who I couldn't help. I didn't think I'd ever get out of there. I know you can't fully understand what it was like—"

"I do."

She squeezed her eyes shut. "You can't—"

"I was taken captive on a mission once."

"What?" She jerked her head up to look at him.

"It was years ago." Something dark moved through his eyes. "It was only a day. A few of us got separated during an attack and snatched by insurgents in the Middle East. They…wanted to make a spectacle out of us. The big, mean UC Navy SEALs weren't so tough when they were stripped naked, tortured, and beaten bloody."

She was rocked to the core. He was so strong, so solid. She couldn't imagine it.

He brushed a hand over her hair. "A team came in and rescued us. The idiots had posted images of us online and they gave away enough landmarks that our teammates could find us." He stroked his thumbs against her cheeks. "Most of the time, they kept us locked in a hole in the ground. Dirt inches from our faces, no fresh air."

She bit her lip at what she heard in his voice. She understood.

"I vowed to myself that when I got free, I'd make the most of my freedom. Of the great outdoors. I learned not to dwell, and take pleasure where I found it."

She arched a brow. "Oh?"

He grinned. "Diving, or riding a bike, or just being in the fresh air. You have a dirty mind, Dr. Vasin." Then his smile faded. "So, I didn't experience being kept for months," his hand slid down her chest, along her scar, "and my scars were nothing like this. But I do understand."

Something tight inside her eased. She pressed her lips to the V of tanned skin at his neck. She knew deep inside that the man standing in front of her would move mountains or cut through the entire alien horde to get to her. "I promise to hold on until you come."

His arms flexed on her and he pressed a quick

kiss to her lips. "Thank you."

"Knowing you'll come for me...I could survive anything knowing that."

He pressed his cheek to her hair. "I'll always come for you, Natalya. Always."

Chapter Eight

She could do this.

Natalya tried to stay calm, but her heart was thumping and her pulse racing. Around her in the quadcopter, Hell Squad was preparing for the mission. They were coiling thin rappelling ropes and clipping carabiners onto their armor.

They'd be rappelling down to the new raptor base. Natalya swallowed back the sick feeling rising in her throat. She'd be in raptor territory. Surrounded by them again.

She closed her eyes, breathing slowly. Her armor felt strange, her body felt hollow, and her new laser pistol felt like it weighed a ton.

"Hey." A warm hand on her shoulder. Ocean waves and sea spray. She looked up at Reed and immediately felt a little calmer.

"You'll do great," he said. "And I'll be by your side the entire time."

She nodded and blew out a breath. "I feel..." *scared out of my brains.* For all her big talk about needing to do this, now she felt like crawling into her bed and never getting out.

He brushed a strand of hair off her temple.

"Being afraid is natural. And it's good. It'll stop you being cocky, taking unnecessary risks."

A hiccupping laugh escaped her. "There is no chance I'll get cocky."

He smiled, turning that rugged face irresistible. "You'll go in there, destroy their energy cubes and show them no one, not even giant invading aliens, can keep you down."

She nodded.

"You've got the cube?"

Another nod. She pulled the blinking alien cube from the mesh bag clipped to her belt and held it up. "Noah helped me and we uploaded the virus. I really wish we could have tested it." But without extra cubes, it just wasn't an option. "I need to set it in place and use my analyzer to finish the last step to activate the virus." Then they'd see if the theory actually worked.

"All right, people, listen up," Marcus' gravelly voice rasped.

He stood at the front of the Hawk, legs spread, looking tough as always.

"This needs to be a quick op. We don't have time to sneak in or take them all out. We need to get in, let Natalya do her stuff, and get out. The Hawk will hover right outside the city hall building for us to rappel down. Head straight for the target. Everyone ready?"

There were nods and murmurs of agreement. Natalya wanted to shout "no way" but she stiffened her spine and shoved the cube back in her bag. She was going to do this.

Marcus' blue eyes glittered. "Ready to go to hell?"

"Hell, yeah!" the team yelled. "The devil needs an ass-kicking!"

The soldiers all pressed buttons on the neck of their armor and lightweight, retractable helmets slid into place.

Natalya blinked and stared at them all. In their black armor and with their focused faces, they looked so...intimidating. But she knew them all now, and under the muscles, the deadly fighting skills, there were men and women who just believed in fighting for what was right.

"Here." Reed's hand slid along her jaw and down to the button on her neckline. Her helmet settled into place.

She looked up at him. She knew he would fight again and again to protect those who needed his help and to fight for freedom.

The riotous emotions in her settled. If Hell Squad could do this every day, she could face her fears and do it once.

Reed held up a carabiner. "Time to hook on." He clipped it to her belt and tested it. "I'm your ride to the ground, brown-eyed girl."

"In any other circumstances, it might be fun," she said.

He tipped her chin up, his thumb running over her lips. "One day, I'll take you rock climbing. Somewhere with crisp mountain air and beautiful scenery as far as we can see."

"Sounds wonderful." She wondered if they would

ever get the chance.

He leaned closer. "And I'll find a patch of wildflowers, lay you down in them and take my time stripping you naked. Then I'll make love to you with just the sunshine on our skin."

Oh. Desire was a hot surge between her legs. "Reed," she whispered quietly.

He grinned and tapped her nose. "Ready?"

Mission. Right. She nodded.

He led her to the side door. Ahead of them, Claudia and Gabe were ready to head out first. Marcus and Cruz would be next, then Reed and Natalya. Shaw would provide cover fire and come down last.

Out the window, she saw the small town the raptors had claimed come into view. It must have been so pretty to live there, nestled amongst the beauty of the Blue Mountains. Now raptor vehicles crowded the streets in front of the shops, and what must have been the town hall. It was an older building, with a wide set of steps up to double doors framed by large columns.

As they got closer, she could make out the raptors wandering the streets, weapons in hand. Her heart thumped again, but she soaked in the reassurance of having Reed by her side.

"They've seen us," Finn, the Hawk pilot, called back from the cockpit.

"Goodie," Shaw said. He sat in the autocannon on the side of the Hawk, swiveling to aim. "Let me say a big hello."

As the autocannon fired, green laser sending the

raptors scrambling, Marcus gave the order to go.

In a graceful move, Claudia and Gabe dived out of the copter, carbines held tightly in their hands.

Natalya's heart leapt into her throat. "Tell me we aren't going out like that."

Reed smoothed a hand over her helmet. "No. They're going in hot and will lay down cover fire for us. Watch Marcus and Cruz."

The other two men went backward, zipping down the sleek, black lines.

Okay, that she could do. Reed pulled her to the very edge of the doorway. Below, she saw the first four Hell Squad members rapidly firing their weapons and running for cover. The raptor weapons were spewing poison around the street in return.

"Time to go." Reed pulled her in front of him.

She was about to ask him if he was going to count to three or something, but he just stepped out of the Hawk, taking her with him.

God. Adrenaline spiked. Air whizzed past her face. They dropped so fast, she felt like she was on an out-of-control carnival ride.

Her feet hit the ground. Reed steadied her, unclipped the hook and then was yanking her toward an overturned SUV.

"We're going to head straight for the steps. Gabe'll go first, so you just follow him. The others will be laying down cover fire. Got it?"

She nodded. But as she studied the path to the building, all she saw were raptors and their ugly green poison arching through the air.

"Look at me." Reed's voice was firm.

She did and was snared by the intensity in the burnished gold.

"You look at Gabe or me. Nothing else. Okay?"

"Okay."

"Right." He touched his earpiece. "Gabe?"

"Ready," the man's deep voice came across the comm.

"Let's do it." Reed pulled her up and they ran.

Natalya just focused on putting one foot in front of the other. Ahead, Gabe charged through the street like an unstoppable linebacker. He shot down aliens, and physically rammed into one or two who got too close. Reed was firing, too.

Just reach the building. She focused on the men. *Reach the building.*

Something exploded to her right, making her scream. Reed grabbed her arm and pulled her forward.

Then they were at the steps.

Gabe took cover behind one of the large columns and Reed tugged her behind a second one. She dared look back and saw the rest of Hell Squad fighting their way toward the building.

Something hit the column, inches from her face, chipping off plaster. She jerked back, heard Reed's curse, and saw three bone-like projectiles embedded in the column.

"Stay in cover," he bit off. "Elle? How many raptors inside?"

"Ten, Reed," came the comm officer's reply. "Most emptied out when you arrived."

Elle sounded incredibly calm. Natalya thought she'd go crazy if she had to listen to the team go through this every day. Especially when one of the men was hers.

"Roger that." Reed eyed Gabe. "When the rest of the team gets here, be ready to go in."

The big man nodded.

Moments later, Marcus and the others sprinted up the stairs. "Let's do this," Marcus said.

With a nod, Gabe unloaded his carbine into the door. Then, with a swift kick, he knocked it in. Claudia moved up beside him. Gabe went in high, and Claudia low.

The sound of carbine fire reverberated through the building. Marcus and Cruz charged forward. Reed urged Natalya to follow.

Inside was a reception area. It had probably been bright and welcoming once, but now, an electronic noticeboard hung crookedly on the wall, its screen cracked. Beside it, the old-fashioned bulletin board was filled with torn and faded posters, their edges curling. The pale-gray carpet had a trail of muddy boot prints stamped into it.

"Through there," Marcus pointed.

Double doors led into the hall. Through them, she had a glimpse of lovely polished wood floors and a stage framed by old red velvet curtains at the back.

But it was all marred by the supplies the raptors had packed into the room.

Green goo splattered the floor near Natalya. She dodged and Reed yanked her out of the line of fire.

She heard the stuff sizzling and knew a tiny touch of it would paralyze. Reed returned fire and around him, the rest of Hell Squad was taking down the remaining raptors.

Then there was silence.

Marcus strode forward. "Gabe, Cruz, get something across the doors. Let's keep any visitors out." His gaze leveled on Natalya and Reed. "Find the energy source. I want this done quickly, and then I want to get out of here before raptor backup arrives."

Reed nodded and together the two of them hurried through the hall. Natalya studied each item they passed. Black boxes filled with…things. Most she couldn't recognize.

When she saw a box overflowing with raw meat, she grimaced. She knew raptors were carnivores, but she really, really didn't want to imagine them tearing into hunks of bloody meat.

No energy cubes.

She released a breath, turning in a circle. "I don't see them."

"They'll be here." Reed was frowning.

Then Natalya spied a cable running along one wall. "Look." She hurried over. It was an ugly thing, spliced with organics, and pulsing lightly.

"Power cable?" Reed asked.

"Possibly." She followed it. It was heading toward the stage area. It ran under the red velvet curtains hanging at the side of the stage.

She pushed the curtains back.

The cable ran right to a pile of energy cubes.

She gasped. *So many.* They were all fitted together, forming a rough pyramid shape about waist-high. They were all operational, pulsing red. She snatched up her analyzer and checked.

"This is it." She pulled her black cube out. She was deciding on the best place to stick it when shouts rang out. Glass smashed and growls filled the room.

She swiveled, heard Reed curse.

Canids were pouring in through the windows high up on the walls. Hell Squad was firing at them. They looked like giant dogs, or wolves, but with scales, sharp spikes on their backs, and jaws filled with sharp teeth.

"Cedar-oil grenades!" someone shouted.

Beside her, she saw Reed pull a slim canister off his belt. "Canid repellent." He pulled his arm back like a baseball player and lobbed the grenade toward the pack of canids. Then he lifted his carbine.

"I'll be right over there, holding them off. Get the cube connected."

With a nod, Natalya focused back on her task. The top of the pile might be best. She had no idea if the location made any difference. She really wished she could scoop all these cubes up and take them back to base to study. She reached up and clicked her cube into place.

Nothing happened. She'd expected...something. She picked up the analyzer, and with a few quick swipes, activated the last bit of code for the virus. She pressed the button.

She waited a few seconds. The howls and snarls of the canids filled her head.

Nothing.

Come on. She frowned and tapped the analyzer screen. The command cube should be communicating with the other cubes, passing along the virus that would burn them out.

But the lights on the pyramid of cubes kept blinking merrily. Like they were laughing at her.

Dammit. She snatched the cube off, knelt, and jammed it onto another at the base of the pile. Still nothing.

Crouched there, the sounds of Hell Squad fighting the canids ringing in her ears, she felt a choking sense of failure creeping in. That horrible, helpless feeling that she knew all too well.

Then she heard a guttural grunt.

She looked up.

From behind the red velvet curtains, a raptor stepped out, his weapon aimed at her head.

Chapter Nine

The terror in Natalya's scream sent an icy chill through Reed.

He spun, and took in the situation in an instant. Horror exploded within him and he charged toward her and the raptor. He was running at full speed, but he already knew he was too far away. "Shaw!" he bellowed.

Out of the corner of his eye, Reed saw the sniper spin, assess the situation in one second flat and lift his rifle.

"Fuck," Shaw shouted. "I don't have a shot. She's in the way."

The raptor loomed, unmoving, over Natalya, making her appear so small and delicate in comparison. Reed had no idea why the bastard was hesitating, but he was thankful. Reed pumped his arms and leapt over a piles of boxes. He had to get to her.

The raptor said something, his words harsh and guttural.

Natalya stayed where she was, frozen. But then she opened her mouth...

And spoke back in raptor.

Reed almost tripped over. He stumbled,

regained his balance, and came to a skidding halt just meters away from her and the raptor. He lifted his carbine, staring down the sights.

"Holy fuck," Shaw whispered.

"For once, I agree with you, Shaw," Claudia murmured in response.

Reed heard a roar in his head, like static. He stepped closer, half his attention on the alien, half on Natalya.

The raptor spoke again, raising his voice.

Natalya spoke in raptor again, then she gasped and stumbled backward. Her hands were splayed against her chest and she hit the floor. Then she started violently flopping around.

Shit, she was having some sort of seizure. Reed aimed his weapon and shot the raptor. The alien's body jolted at the laser hit. The rest of Reed's team opened fire, too.

Then he ran to Natalya's side. His hands hesitated over her for a second, but one look at her pale face, her convulsing body, and he grabbed her. He laid her flat.

"Claudia?" He looked up. "You got something to stop this?"

The soldier stared at him for a second, before she nodded and hurried forward. Seconds later, she was injecting Natalya with a drug to stop the seizures.

Come on. He cupped her head to stop it hitting the floor. After what felt like an eternity, the violent shudders slowed and she went limp.

"The cube didn't work." Marcus was scowling

ANNA HACKETT

and eyeing Natalya like she was a threat. Then he crouched and snatched the cube that had fallen from her hand.

Reed slid his arms under her and stood, cradling her to his chest.

"Marcus?" Elle's voice. "Two inbound raptor patrols. And it looks like they're mobilizing nearby troops. You need to get out of there."

"We haven't achieved the mission...and Natalya..."

"I heard." Elle's voice was grim. "General Holmes is sending in a Sentinel."

Marcus cursed. "We're going to bomb the place?"

Reed knew the large Sentinel bomber drone carried a lot of fire power. It wouldn't leave anything behind but a small crater.

"Yes. This location is too close to Blue Mountain Base. The general says we can't risk it."

"Fine." Marcus motioned with his carbine. "Hell Squad. Let's get out of here."

Reed strode outside, hitching Natalya's body higher in his arms. She was so motionless, it worried him. But what worried him more was what had happened inside.

The Hawk touched down in the middle of the street. They hurried aboard and moments later, the Hawk took off.

No one spoke.

Reed sat with Natalya in his arms, and all around him his squad was silent, watching her like she was a bomb about to detonate.

The tense ride was over quickly. The huge doors

covering the Hawk landing pads retracted, and soon the copter was lowering through the rock tunnel. The skids hit the pads.

Marcus slid the door open, his face more serious than usual. "Reed—"

He was about to respond when he saw General Holmes outside the Hawk. With an armed security team.

Oh, God. Reed felt a rush of hot, scalding emotion run through him. His arms tightened around Natalya. He was a soldier, and he knew exactly how many men, women and children called the base home. And he knew he'd vowed to protect them from any threat.

But for the first time, he was torn by his duty.

He stepped out and was grateful when his team flanked him.

"I'm sorry, Reed," the general said. "We need to take Natalya into custody for now. For everyone's safety."

One of the base security members stepped forward. He was holding a set of shock cuffs.

Reed stiffened. "Sir, she was locked up for months in that lab. And she's hurt. The restraints aren't necessary."

General Holmes' eyes flashed with sorrow...but they were also filled with a resigned resoluteness. "Again, I'm sorry. But they are."

Natalya stirred. "Reed? What happened?"

"We made it out." He gently set her on her feet. He felt trapped—like he was pinned down by the enemy with no place to go. "Natalya, do you remember what you said to the raptor back there, in the town?"

Her brow furrowed. She was absently rubbing her chest. "I...I'm not really sure. I think I told him to back off and leave me alone."

Reed closed his eyes for a second. "You spoke in raptor."

"What?" She gave a nervous laugh. "I don't speak raptor." She looked around, seeing all the others watching her. She ran her hands up and down her arms, tension filling her face. "No...that's not possible."

"Natalya, you need to come with these men," General Holmes said.

It was then she saw the cuffs. She blanched. "No."

"I'm sorry, but I have to insist."

She shook her head violently. "No. I'm not a raptor. I'm not one of them." She looked at Reed, her gaze imploring. "Reed, please?" Then her gaze sharpened on his face and she stiffened. "You believe me, right?"

Hell, he didn't know what he thought. "Look—"

"No!" She twisted away from him. "No. You can't lock me up. Not again." She lunged away from the crowd.

The security guards grabbed her, each holding an arm. She twisted and kicked like a wild animal.

Something in Reed broke. He stepped forward, but strong arms grabbed him. Cruz and Marcus held him in place.

"Let me go."

Marcus leaned in, murmuring low next to his ear. "You attack them now, you won't be able to help her later. Understand?"

When Natalya started screaming, a high, wild sound, Reed growled. His entire body quivered with the urge to attack. They couldn't do this to her. It would break her.

"Here." Doc Emerson bustled in, an iono-stretcher hovering behind her. "Put her on here."

The two guards maneuvered Natalya onto the stretcher. The doc was murmuring soothing word, but Natalya's eyes were wide and panicked. She was too far gone in her terror to be soothed.

With a sad, resigned look on her face, the doc pulled a strap from the side of the stretcher and secured Natalya's wrist down.

She made a cry like a wounded animal. Reed closed his eyes, his hands clenched into fists. Then Emerson strapped the other wrist down.

Natalya's eyes caught his. In them, he saw terror…and betrayal.

Emerson pressed a pressure injector to the side of Natalya's neck. A second later, his brown-eyed girl went limp.

As they took her away, Reed cursed and pulled away from his team. *Fuck*. Just fuck.

***

Shaking hard, Natalya paced across the room.

They'd locked her in a cell. In the prison area.

Oh, there were no bars, but that didn't make it

any less confining. She glanced at the large glass window she couldn't see through. She knew the one-way mirror was reinforced so even a raptor couldn't get through it. Clenching her hands together, she turned and kept pacing. She also knew there was a raptor down here, in one of the cells.

How could she have spoken the raptor language? She curled her fists up to her chest. She felt so alone. What she remembered most was watching Reed's face as she'd been dragged away. He hadn't helped her.

She spun away and paced again. This all had to be a mistake.

The door open and she turned.

A redheaded woman stepped through. She was tall and fit, and wearing a neatly pressed blue uniform. Captain Laura Bladon—head of the detention area and Interrogation team. She had a face that gave nothing away as she eyed Natalya for a second. Then she waved someone in. "Five minutes, that's it."

Reed stepped inside, and Captain Bladon closed the door firmly behind him.

He stepped forward, hand outstretched. "Natalya—"

She stumbled backward until her back pressed against the wall. "Don't touch me."

His face hardened and his hand fell to his side. "I'm sorry."

"For what?" she spat. "For letting them take me?" The rational part of her knew he couldn't have stopped them, but dammit, he could have tried.

"Sweetheart—"

Something inside her crumpled. "You let them take me." A sob tried to break free from her chest but she ruthlessly pushed it down. "I'm a prisoner again. There's no fresh air in here, Reed."

He closed his eyes. "You spoke raptor, Natalya. It freaked everyone out."

Anger spiked. "I survived *four* months with those aliens torturing me! All I've done since I've been here is try to heal and try to help. And this is what I get?"

"No one is asking for anything, except answers." Something slid through his gaze before he hid it.

"What?" she demanded.

"Nothing. I need—"

"Just tell me, Reed. There's something else, isn't there?"

He released a breath. "Dammit. There are some questions about why the cube didn't work."

Her eyes widened. "They think I did it on purpose? To help the animals who cut me open?"

Reed held out a hand. "I know that isn't true, but because of the hybrids who got in here before, people are spooked."

"Including you." She wrapped her arms around herself. She'd thought she'd been heading back toward normal: getting healthy again, working, contemplating taking Reed MacKinnon as her lover.

Now it had all been crushed. Nothing but dust.

He cursed and strode toward her. She held out a hand to fend him off. "Stay back."

"Never." His tone was firm as steel. He wrapped his arms around her, holding her as she struggled.

He tangled his hands in her short hair and tugged until she was forced to look at him.

"I'm sorry, baby. I'm sorry I couldn't fight them all off, or do *something*. But I'll get you out of here. We'll work this out. I know you, Natalya. I've seen your beauty, your strength. And you're mine."

His mouth slammed down on hers. For a second, she kept struggling, the pain in her needing to lash out at him.

But then the force of his kiss, the almost brutal heat of it, sucked her in. It was real, honest, something she could trust. Natalya threw her arms around him and kissed him back. She stopped thinking and just let herself feel.

They pulled apart, both of them panting.

"I'm sorry," he murmured again.

The hurt part of her still trembled.

"I'm sorry." His hands tightened on her. "However many times you need me to say it, I will."

Deep down, she knew there hadn't been anything he could have done. And he was here now.

"We'll work this out." His hands cupped her cheeks. "But I want to say it now, I don't care what we discover. You're mine. End of story."

She wanted to believe it would be that easy. She wanted to curl up in his strong arms and let him shelter her from the world.

But that wasn't a choice. And even if it was, she

couldn't hide behind him.

Still, when his hand slid down and grabbed hers, his fingers entwining with hers, a spark lit inside her. Maybe he could at least stand by her side.

"Trust me?" he murmured.

She thought again of how she'd felt when they'd dragged her away from him. Of watching him look confused and torn. This man had the power to destroy her.

But he'd always been there for her. Right from the moment he'd carried her out of that raptor lab. She nodded.

He let out a relieved breath and dropped a kiss to the top of her head. "Okay. Now, you need to listen to me. I know you won't like this…but you need to let Emerson examine you."

Natalya's gut clenched, her fingers jerking on his.

"I know." His voice softened. "I know it sucks, I know you don't want any more tests and scans, but please let her check you out."

Natalya stayed still for a moment. God, the thought of being flat on an examination bed, lights shining in her eyes, needles sliding into her skin…it left her dry-mouthed and terrified.

But she had to get this cleared up. She wasn't a raptor hybrid, *dammit*. "You'll stay with me?"

He squeezed her hand. "Every step of the way."

Chapter Ten

Reed watched Natalya as she tried to fight down a panic attack. She was lying on a bed in the infirmary, clutching his hand. Her breathing was too fast and her gaze kept skipping around the room, not settling on anything for longer than a couple of seconds.

Hell, she'd been through so much and now they—*humans*—were subjecting her to this.

"It's okay, brown-eyed girl." He leaned forward, his lips brushing her ear. He kept his voice low, just for her. "When this is done, we'll head to our private little pool." He nipped the lobe of her ear, almost smiled when she jumped. "I plan on getting you very naked."

She licked her lips and turned her head toward him. "Then what?"

"Then you better be ready, because I'm going to fuck you...hard."

"Reed..." Her voice was breathy.

She'd stopped shaking, so he guessed his distraction was working. He stroked a hand down her arm. "I've got so many things I'm going to do to you. I've spent a lot of time thinking about them."

She smiled at him and damned if Reed didn't

feel like he'd won some sort of prize.

Doc Emerson bustled in, her lab coat flapping around her. "All right, Natalya. You don't have to worry about anything."

But Natalya instantly stiffened. Reed swallowed his frustration and nodded at the doctor.

"I'm going to do a scan. It's a 3-D resonance scan. I will need to inject you with a special dye, but after that, no more poking or prodding, I promise."

Natalya was fingering the top of her scar. "Then what?"

"The dye works its way through your body, and then the scanner can project a 3-D image for me to study."

Natalya pulled in a long breath. "Okay."

Reed held her hand while Emerson slid a needle in Natalya's arm. Then the doc swung a boxy-looking scanner over the bed, starting it at Natalya's feet. Natalya didn't move an inch, her jaw clenched. Her gaze locked resolutely on the ceiling.

"Okay, the first image should be coming up soon." Emerson adjusted something on the scanner. As the machine slowly moved up Natalya's body, images appeared in the air above.

Wow. Reed couldn't believe the detail. He could see the veins, muscles, bones, everything inside her. Emerson used a gloved hand to turn the three-dimensional image and zoom in on certain things.

The scanner finished with Natalya's legs and inched up over her pelvis and stomach.

Emerson's brow was scrunched as she stared at the scans. Every now and then she turned the scan or isolated a single organ or structure. "Everything looks fine, Natalya. You're doing a great job."

The scanner moved up over her chest.

Emerson stiffened a little. Natalya didn't notice it, but Reed did. He frowned at the picture in the air. There was too much on it, lungs, ribs...he couldn't see if anything was out of the ordinary.

Emerson tapped the screen and just one organ appeared.

She gasped and Reed blinked. It...*hell*, he didn't know what it was. It was an ugly, misshapen mass of alien tissue covered with a lattice of tiny black veins. It pulsed, contracting rhythmically.

Natalya went stiff as a board. "What is that?"

"I..." Emerson's gaze caught Reed's, helplessness in her eyes. "It's your heart."

"That is *not* a heart," Natalya said, her voice high-pitched and reedy.

Holy shit. Reed watched the organ, the heart, beating a little faster than a regular heartbeat.

Emerson cleared her throat. "It's a raptor heart. They must have transplanted it into you."

"No!" Natalya sat up and pushed the scanner away. The scan image flickered and disappeared. The scanner fell over, crashing to the floor. "Take it out. I want you to take it out."

Emerson took a steadying breath. "I—"

"Take it out!" The last word was a scream.

"Hey." Reed kept his hand on hers. "Stay calm."

"I can't. I want it out."

He yanked her off the bed and into his lap. He subdued her when she struggled until she was nestled against his chest. "I'm here. You aren't alone and this changes nothing. Got it?"

Something in his tone must have got through. She stared at his face then slowly turned back to look at Emerson.

"I can't remove it, Natalya," the doctor said. "I'd need a donor heart or a synthetic one and I don't have either. I'll do some more tests—"

Natalya went rigid.

Emerson scraped a hand through her hair. "Look, I know it isn't what you want to hear, but that…heart…is pumping. It's doing the job of a human heart. You're healthy. From what I can tell from your scan results, your DNA is clear and there is no trace of the orange transformation fluid that seems to be a necessary part of turning a human into a raptor."

"Why did I speak raptor, then?"

"I'm not sure. There may be some latent abilities from the raptor organ. Perhaps they have some sort of genetic memory. I will investigate more, but for now, all I can tell you is that I am ninety-nine percent certain you aren't turning into a raptor."

A shiver wracked Natalya and Reed held her tighter.

She gave a nod. Then her hands slid down over his, and she pulled his hands away from her. "Reed? Would you do something for me?"

"Anything."

Her gaze ran over his face, like she was

memorizing his features. "I need some time alone."

***

Reed picked at his dinner. Sounds of the dining room echoed around him—cutlery clinking against plates, happy conversations, laughter.

His squadmates surrounded him, everyone eating as well, but no one was saying a word.

Natalya had a raptor heart inside her. *Shit.*

"I can't stand this any longer." Claudia set her knife and fork down. "You haven't said a thing, Reed. How the hell is she?"

He pushed his plate away. "She's shaken, scared."

"Doc work out why the hell she could speak the raptor language?" Shaw asked.

Reed ground his teeth together. "Why not just ask? Is she a hybrid?"

Shaw lifted his drink and took a sip. "I know she isn't a hybrid, man. She's been here weeks. Never seen any sign she was a raptor."

Reed ran a hand over his face. "She has a raptor heart."

Shaw frowned. "Come again?"

"Those bastards cut her open, removed her heart and slapped one of their own ugly organs in her."

A hushed silence fell.

"Fucking hell," Shaw said.

"That's—" Claudia just shook her head.

Marcus scowled. "Fucking raptors."

"The doc says it's working fine, like a normal

heart, but that maybe it also gives her some…raptor-like abilities. They'll have to do more tests." He shoved his chair back. It was one of those times he felt like the walls of the base were closing in on him. "And Natalya wanted some time alone."

"Alone?" Claudia's brows rose to her hairline. "And you bought that? She needs you. You leaving her alone just reinforces whatever fucked up thoughts are spinning through her head. It tells her that you don't want to be with her right now."

Reed blinked. Was that really what Natalya thought? He'd thought he was doing the right thing, honoring her request. *Hell.* He shot to his feet and left the dining room at a run.

He made it through the tunnels to her quarters in record time. He thumped a fist against her door and waited.

No answer.

But a locked door was no match for him. It took him a few seconds to hack the electronic lock and open the door.

Her quarters were empty. He strode through, the sense of emptiness slapping him in the face. He headed over to her bed, and noticed her narrow closet was open. Some items of clothing were strewn on the floor, and the rest of the cabinet was empty. His jaw tightened. He poked his head into the bathroom. The same thing. Toiletries yanked out of the cupboard littering her sink.

Dammit. She was gone.

Reed charged through the tunnels. He grabbed his communicator.

"Steele," a gravelly voice answered.

"Marcus, she's gone. She's run."

Marcus used one of his creative curses. "Call Noah, get him to check the security feed. Then call Devlin Gray. I hear he's a hell of a tracker."

"Thanks." Reed ended the call and made another, changing direction at the same time and heading down another tunnel.

"What?" A cranky male voice.

"Noah, Reed here. Natalya's done a runner. Can you check the security feed, tell me which exit she used?"

"Shit," Noah muttered. "Yeah. Give me a minute."

"Thanks." Reed reached the door he wanted but before he could knock, it opened.

Devlin Gray stood there, a brow arched. He was tall and lean, with dark hair and equally dark eyes. He was dressed in dark trousers and a crisp white shirt. The few times Reed had seen him, he'd always thought the guy looked like he'd just walked out of a dinner party or a boardroom.

"Natalya, Dr. Vasin, she's left. She's messed up about what happened, scared—" Reed's voice hitched and he looked up, taking a deep breath. When he focused back on Devlin, sympathy shifted over the man's sharp features. "She's alone, out there. I heard from Marcus that you're a hell of a tracker."

Devlin gave one short nod, stepped into the tunnel and pulled his door closed behind him. "I'll help you find her."

Reed's communicator beeped. "Noah?"

"The westernmost exit. She took the tunnel to the surface."

"Got it. Thanks. I owe you." He slipped his communicator back into his pocket. "Western exit. Come on."

Together, Reed and Devlin made it to the western exit and out of the tunnel into the night air. Devlin glanced slowly around, like he was soaking in the atmosphere.

Even though a desperate, edgy tension was pounding through Reed, he stepped back and stayed quiet. Santha had mentioned before that Devlin could track a mosquito through a swamp. Reed had to trust the man could find Natalya.

Devlin crouched, pressing his fingers to the soft, grass-covered earth. Then he nodded toward the trees. "She went that way."

"You can tell?"

Devlin raised a brow, then stood in one smooth move. "She's wearing size seven shoes, and carrying a small bag. Yeah, I can tell."

As they moved into the trees, Reed clicked on the heavy-duty flashlight he'd brought with him. He couldn't let himself think about what she was feeling, what was going through her mind, and just where the hell she thought she was going. He just had to find her first...and bring her home.

They jogged through the trees. Every now and then, Dev would stop and finger a leaf on a tree or touch something only he could see on the ground.

"Where'd you learn to track?" Reed asked.

"In the African Kalahari."

Reed waited a beat, thinking the man would elaborate.

When Devlin remained silent, Reed rolled his eyes. "Okay, how'd you end up in the Kalahari, learning to track?"

Devlin paused. "I was on a…mission. It went bad. I was double-crossed by a fellow agent and got dumped in the middle of the desert a long way from civilization." He was silent for a moment. "I was out of water and just about dead when some local Bushmen found me. The San people."

Reed couldn't even imagine it.

"They nursed me back to health. I stayed with them for a few months. After what had happened…I guess I wasn't in a rush to head home. I ended up spending time with their hunters, learned how to track, how to find water, how to survive in the desert."

"Sounds like a hell of a vacation." Reed suspected the truth was a lot deeper and darker than Devlin was letting on.

"Yeah. Well, a few months later I figured it was time to head back to reality. I made my way to the Namibian capital, Windhoek. From there, I called…my employer."

Reed was curious what the man's exact background was, but he stopped himself from asking. If Devlin wanted to share his secrets, he would. For now, the man was helping him find Natalya and Reed didn't want to repay him with questions.

"Dr. Vasin seems like a nice woman. I was sorry to hear what the raptors had done to her," Devlin said.

Reed's mouth flattened. "Yeah. She's been through a lot."

"And you're helping her come out the other side?"

"Damn straight. She's mine now, I'm not letting her deal with this alone." Or get away from him, either.

Devlin gave him an approving nod. "When someone's walked in darkness...they need a strong hand to pull them out." Suddenly, Devlin frowned and crouched to study the ground.

Reed watched, his nerves stretching tight.

After a couple of minutes, Dev stood. "*Dammit.*"

"What?" Reed asked.

"Lost her." The lean man walked in a circle. "Shine the light on the ground."

Reed obeyed. He searched for any sign, any clue to where she'd gone. He was worried as hell. She was upset, alone, out in the bush. But a deeper part of him was also pissed.

She'd left him.

"Ah, got her." Dev fingered a branch of a medium-sized bush, clearly seeing something Reed couldn't. "This way." The man set off again.

They'd traveled a fair distance from base when the surroundings started to look familiar. Reed narrowed his gaze on a fallen tree, with its thick, rotting trunk. Something inside him burst free. "I know where she's going."

"You sure?"

Reed nodded. The waterhole was only another hundred meters or so through the trees. They'd just come at it from a different direction than Reed usually used. "Yeah."

Devlin nodded and shoved his hands in his pockets. "All right, then. Guess I should wish you luck?"

"I'll take it."

Devlin inclined his head. "Good hunting." Then he slipped into the shadows and silently disappeared.

Right. Reed faced in the direction of the pool. Time to get his woman back.

He flicked off his light and stepped out onto the edge of the waterhole.

He didn't see anything, or hear anything. The surface of the water looked perfectly still in the moonlight. *Damn.* What if he'd missed her? What if she'd left? It felt like a hand gripped his lungs and squeezed. What if he'd lost her?

Then he heard a splash of water.

He stepped closer, his boots hitting rock.

And saw her.

She rose out of the water like a sensuous nymph in a spring. Her slender back was to him, crossed with tiny black bikini strings, her skin glowing in the moonlight.

One word reverberated through Reed. *Mine.*

Chapter Eleven

Natalya wasn't sure what made her turn around. There hadn't been any sound. Just a whisper of sensation on her skin, like the brush of a cool night breeze.

Then she saw him standing there. A big, dark shadow at the edge of the pool.

His hands were clenched into fists at his side, his body rigid, and she felt the anger pumping off him.

She sank down in the water. She should have just left. She shouldn't have come here, to their private place, for one last swim. A personal goodbye to the man she would have given her heart to…if she'd had one.

"You were leaving? Just like that?"

His words hit her like bullets. Oh, he was really mad. "It wasn't an easy decision—"

"And you didn't have the guts to tell me?

She stirred, the water rippling around her. Her own emotions rose up, everything she'd been through coalescing into a hot ball of hurt. "This is more for your benefit. I'm not human, Reed."

He made a scoffing sound, stepping forward until his feet were right at the edge of the pool.

"You think what they did to you makes you less human?"

"I have a raptor heart!" Her yelled words echoed through the trees, scaring some nocturnal bird from its perch on the branches. "I—" Her voice cracked and she felt tears sliding down her cheeks.

Reed moved and through her blurry vision, she saw him tear his shirt off over his head. She blinked, and even in her turmoil, the sight of dappled moonlight on all those hard muscles made her flush. He shoved his trousers down with one fast push, kicked off his shoes, and then he dived from the edge in a smooth, practiced move, cutting cleanly through the water.

He rose right in front of her, water sliding off him. Then his arms were circling her, the heat of him warming her.

With a choked sob, she grabbed him and held on. The angry, shocked, and ugly emotions in her burst and she started crying. Nothing elegant, or pretty, but hard, broken sobs.

And he held her, rocking her a little, and murmuring nonsense words to her.

She gripped him, her fingers curling into hard muscle. "I wanted to be normal. Like I was before. I was confident, Reed, sure of myself and my position in the world."

He tucked her head in under his chin, her face pressed to his neck. He was treading water easily, keeping them both afloat. "You can't be normal. And it has nothing to do with what's in your chest. I'm not the same person I was before those insurgents locked me in that hole in the ground. They may not have implanted anything in me, but I still carry that experience. I'm not the same person I was before Jo, either. Or before the aliens came and blew the world to hell. None of us are."

Natalya bit down on her lip and tried to breathe. "It's not the same. The raptors left something in me, something physical. A piece of them...and I can't get rid of it."

"Whether it's a physical or emotional scar, it doesn't matter, Natalya. We'll always carry something with us. It's what we choose to do to move forward that counts."

It couldn't be that simple. She wanted to believe she could move forward, but the scar on her chest and the beat that echoed in her ears wouldn't let her.

A hand fisted in her wet hair. Hot gold eyes seared her. "We can't go back, sweetheart. Only forward. I want you to move forward with me."

Her stomach clenched. "How can you still want me?"

He muttered a curse and shifted her, urging her to wrap her legs around his hips. She was wearing a black bikini she'd found at the clothing store. Something a little sexy and daring, with ties at the side. At the time, she'd daydreamed of teasing Reed with it.

He moved her and she felt the hard press of his cock against her. She gasped.

"Yeah. I want you. I've wanted you a really long time and it's got nothing to do with whatever pumps the blood around your body."

She blinked. When he put it like that...

"It's got to do with the strength I see in you. A quiet core of steel. I've seen you fighting to recover, fighting to help by using that crazy smart mind of yours, and I certainly haven't missed those lovely curves of yours. The way those teasing little skirts hug your hips drives me crazy."

She blinked again. "Those skirts are...ordinary. Sensible."

Another male scoffing noise. "Hell no, my brown-eyed girl. They've been like a red flag to me. They make me want to shove them up and put my mouth between your legs."

"Reed." She moved against him. She felt so empty, so hollow, and she knew he was the only thing that could fill her up.

"I need you on my cock, Natalya." He moved through the water, carrying them to the edge. "I want to slide inside you and make you mine."

God. Her blood was pounding through her. "Yes." She moved her hips again, that hard bulge rubbing against where she was rapidly growing very wet. Need was a strong potent thing.

He fingered the tiny bikini top, sliding a thumb under the strap. "This little thing is designed to drive me crazy, right? I can see the perfect swells of your pretty breasts, but those rosy nipples are hidden from me. Tease." He yanked the top off and tossed it up on the bank.

Then he lowered his head and sucked.

Oh. She arched up into his mouth, her hands

delving into the gold-tipped strands of his hair. She pulled him closer. "More. Harder." She needed him, too.

"Greedy." He sucked harder, making her cry out. Then he switched to her other breast.

While he was licking and sucking, his other hand slid down. He fingered the ties at the side of her bikini bottoms, but he left them tied up and fingered the edge close to where she was wet and needy. He slid a finger under the side, teasing a little, then he touched her.

"Reed!" She surged against him. The dual sensations of his mouth and fingers were too much. But she needed more, oh, she needed so much more.

"Mmm, so hot and wet for me here." His finger slid inside her, making her moan.

"I'm so empty, Reed. Please."

"Oh, yeah." He slid another finger inside her. "So, tight, baby. You're going to feel so damn good around my cock." He pulled out of her, then impatiently tore the bikini bottoms off. "I'm going to fill you up."

He spun her and pressed her toward the smooth, flat rock at the edge of the pool. Her breasts pressed against the firm surface. The rock still retained a little warmth from the day and the sensation against her nipples was electrifying.

A big hand pushed her knees apart, then his hand was sliding up against her wetness. "Brown-eyed girl, I'm going to fuck you in my bunk later. With all the lights on. I want to see every inch of you. Moonlight is beautiful on your skin, but I want to see these sweet, plump lips."

God, she hadn't guessed he'd talk dirty during sex. It was driving her wild. But she wanted to make sure he didn't think he was the only one on this ride. She was a full participant, not just holding on and letting him drive. She reached back until her fingers brushed his cock. It was hard, thick, rising high.

"I have some things I want to explore, too." A naughtiness she'd never felt rose up inside of her. She licked her lips and looked back over her shoulder. "I want to taste you, suck you and feel you in my throat."

"Fuck, Natalya." His hips surged forward, thrusting his hard length into her hand. "Damn, you're going to make me spill all over your fingers." He tugged her hand away and urged her back onto the rock. "Later, baby. Later I'll slide my hands into that pixie hair of yours and watch you suck my cock. But right now—"

She felt the head of his cock brush between her legs. Anticipation coiled in her belly.

"Right now, I'm going to thrust inside you and keep going until you come."

She shoved back against him. "Do it."

He plunged forward.

God. He filled her up, stretching unused muscles.

He pulled out, then thrust back in. "Damn, baby, you feel so good. So tight, so warm."

She moaned. As he started moving in a steady

rhythm, she felt every nerve ending overload with sensation.

"Natalya." His hands gripped her hips. "All mine. You aren't running away from me. Wherever you go, I'll find you. Got it?"

"Yes." A breathy whisper. She felt her orgasm growing, a huge thing she knew would hurt as much as it felt good.

"Damn, I wish I had more light, wish I could see you stretched around me." He thrust harder, faster. "For now, I'll focus on how you feel when you come. Ready?"

"Yes, yes." She'd take whatever this man had to give her, because raptor heart or not, she was already falling in love with him.

***

Reed tightened one hand on Natalya's hip, holding her in place as he slammed home. God, the sight of her pale skin in the moonlight, her upturned ass, it made the need in him ratchet up another notch. He felt her body tightening and knew her release was coming.

He slid a palm up her back to rest on her shoulder blades. He kept pumping into her.

"Reed." Her palms were splayed against the rock, like she was searching for something to anchor herself.

"Let go, baby. I've got you."

Her orgasm hit. She screamed, arching her back. He held her in place and kept thrusting. God, she was beautiful. She tightened on him, milking his cock. *Damn.* He gritted his teeth. He couldn't hold on.

His release hit him like a Hawk at high speed. It slammed into him and he gripped her tighter, pouring inside her.

Panting, his body still shuddering, he dropped down and covered her with his body, their legs still in the water. He turned her a little, so he wasn't squashing her and so he could move his hand over her chest, over her beating heart.

"Don't care what they did. That's on them, not you." He traced a circle over the fast beat, hard enough to make his point. "That thing is giving you a pulse, life, but *I* made it race like this. And I want to keep doing that."

"Reed," she murmured. "You make my knees weak when you talk like that." She gave a little laugh. "Although, so does the dirty talk during sex. I'd never guessed that you'd say things like you did."

He shifted against her, his half-erect cock sliding against her, eliciting a moan. "And I never guessed my prim scientist would like it so much, or do a little of her own."

She laughed again and it was a free, easy sound that made him feel light.

"Come on, beautiful. Let's get back to base."

She stiffened a little, reality leaking in.

"Nuh-uh." He drew back and then pulled her up. He twisted her to face him. "Don't let the bad back in. Forward. That's what we have to focus on."

"Forward. The future." She gave a determined nod. "Okay."

"And, my brown-eyed girl, I can tell you that your future involves more hot, mind-blowing sex."

Her teeth flashed white in the darkness. She cupped one of his stubble-covered cheeks. "I never realized former Navy SEALs were so bossy. But I like it."

***

Holy fuck, he was going to come just watching her.

Reed sat on the edge of his bunk, naked, with Natalya on her knees in front of him. She was cupping his cock in slim hands, her eyes alight, her cheeks flushed.

As he'd promised, all the lights were on. He'd already fucked her in the shower and in his bed. Now, she was having a little fun.

And the tease was wearing one of her skirts and a white shirt. And he was well aware she had nothing on underneath. He could see the shadow of her nipples against the white fabric and his hard-as-a-rock cock was well aware that all he had to do was slip that skirt up and find her wet for him.

She moved closer, one hand on his thigh to steady herself. She opened her red lips and all thoughts flew out of Reed's head. *Damn*. He had to focus on not coming too soon.

She teased him, swirling her tongue around the head of his cock. Her cheeks flushed a pretty pink, and it was nice to see her just enjoying herself. His muscles twisted into tight knots of anticipation. She licked down his cock, making little humming noises as she did. Damn, she was *really* enjoying herself.

She moved back up and then, without any warning, sucked him into her mouth.

"Natalya." He groaned, his hands clamping on the edge of the bed.

She made that humming noise again, bobbing up and down on him, and this time the vibration made him groan. She worked her way lower, taking more and more of him into her mouth.

"That's it, baby. You can take all of me."

She did, relaxing and swallowing him down.

"I'm going to come." His hands went to her head, holding her there as he pushed into her mouth with short, firm strokes.

She moaned around him, her big brown eyes on his face, and a second later, his orgasm—a fucking intense one—tore through him. His groan was long and loud. He spurted into her warm mouth and watched as she licked the last of it from her lips. She smiled at him.

Reed had never seen anything more beautiful. He gripped her chin. "Every time I look at you, you steal my breath."

Her smile dissolved, need in her eyes. "Reed."

He tugged her up and kissed her. It went from tender to hot in a flash. He rolled, pinning her to the bed, but he forced himself to cool it a little.

He'd been rough with her, hard. He wanted to give her the tenderness, too. To show her how good slow and lazy could be as well.

Gripping the hem of her skirt he shoved it up.

"Let me undo the zipper," she said.

"Nope. Leave it there."

Her mouth opened, her brown eyes glowing. "Want me to wear my glasses?"

He growled, leaned down and nipped her lip. "Next time."

He undid her top button. Now her face changed, nerves skittering.

The next button followed. "No secrets between us. I don't give a flying fuck about this scar or what you think it represents. To me, it's still a symbol of courage and survival." He flicked open her shirt.

As he'd done before, he leaned down and kissed the scar, tracing it with his lips.

Her hands tangled in his hair. "You are so gorgeous, like a big, healthy lion on the prowl. A part of me thinks you deserve a normal, complete woman."

He nipped at her with his teeth. "Don't say that." His tone was firm, unyielding. "Ever again. I deserve you. I want you. And I'm taking you."

When he slid inside her, he did it slowly. He watched the expressions flicker across her face and, as he moved inside her, the two of them joined as one, he vowed he'd fight anyone who tried to keep her from him. Even herself.

Chapter Twelve

Walking into the dining room for lunch the next day, Natalya felt a rush of nerves. By now, most of the base would have heard that she'd spoken raptor, been imprisoned, and dragged off to the infirmary. In the close confines of the base, gossip was rife. She forced herself to keep her head held high and not to squeeze Reed's hand like a lifeline.

They had spent a lazy morning in bed, laughing, making love. He'd fed her breakfast in bed...and her toast had ended up squashed beneath her as they'd fed on each other, instead.

They stepped into the middle of the lunch crowd. Conversations stopped, cutlery rattled onto plates...silence.

Reed glowered. God, it was one thing to not want people to stare at her, but she *really* didn't want them treating Reed like a pariah.

Swallowing, she took a step backward.

"Good afternoon." Claudia appeared beside Natalya, gripping her elbow gently, but firmly. "We're sitting over here."

Shaw bustled up on the other side of Reed and slapped him on the back. "Man, I see you somehow convinced this super-smart lady to take you on." A gusty sigh. "Almost all the good women are taken."

Claudia snorted. "Shaw, you never keep the same woman longer than a night."

He shrugged. "Someone has to keep the single ladies company." He waggled his eyebrows at Natalya. "But a man can dream."

Natalya blinked, overcome with emotion as the pair herded them past the gawkers over to a table against the far wall. All of Hell Squad was there, along with Santha, Elle, and even young Bryony. The girl waved, bouncing in her seat. She was wearing a set of dog tags and had two pink hair clips in her short, dark hair.

Marcus stood and pushed out two seats beside him. "Glad you managed to pull yourself out of bed, MacKinnon."

Reed helped Natalya into a chair, smiling at his boss. She was thankful to see the tension in him lessen. "Well, my bed was warm, and soft and just too darn tempting."

Natalya knew her cheeks were pink.

Shaw sat and snatched up a piece of toast with what looked like black grease smeared on it. "Heard Navy SEALs were lazy. Now I have proof."

Reed snorted and sat down beside her. "And I heard Aussie SAS grunts think they're tough because they eat that disgusting stuff." He nodded at Shaw's toast.

"Vegemite is like a sixth food group, mate. But I'll grant you, it's not for the faint of heart. It's an acquired taste."

Claudia sat back in her chair. "A bit like you, then."

Shaw gave her an evil grin. "You love me, Frost."

She huffed out a breath and snatched up a glass of juice. "In your dreams, Baird."

Elle set a plate of food down in front of Natalya. "Eat. You probably need the energy." A small knowing smile played around her lips.

More heat rushed into Natalya's cheeks, but she picked up her fork and started eating the substitute eggs. She was hungry.

Conversations slowly started again, and after a while, she tuned out the interested stares and quiet whispers. Hell Squad helped.

They were all talking at once. Ribbing each other, talking about weapons and vehicles, rehashing old missions. Bryony was telling big bad Gabe about what she was learning in school and the scary man appeared to be listening with apparent interest.

They were like a big family—albeit with more muscles and tattoos and training in ways to kill people. But she was grateful for their support.

Suddenly a wave of titters flared in the crowd. She glanced up and saw Noah bearing down on them. He was scowling, and glaring at anyone whose gaze he caught. He had his dark hair tied at the back of his neck, highlighting his hawkish features.

He stopped at the table. "Hey, Natalya. How are you doing?"

She nodded. "I'm doing okay."

"Couldn't believe it when I heard they'd locked you up. Insanity." He cast a dark glance around the room. "And I'm sure all these fu—" his gaze dropped to Bryony "—idiots are gossiping up a storm. Morons wouldn't have their precious hot water if it wasn't for you. And how do they show their thanks? At the first instant, they doubt you, talk about you behind your back, make someone who's already survived hell relive it again."

The room went quiet. Natalya squeezed Reed's hand and stood. She gripped Noah's arm. "Thank you. I'm so grateful you believe in me. But you don't have to punish them. They've survived their own versions of hell, too, and I know they have loved ones they want to keep safe. They're just scared. It hurts, but I understand."

"Glad you do," he grumped. Then he sat down, reached over and plucked some bacon substitute off Elle's plate. "I've been working on that cube. I think I know why it didn't work."

"Oh, yeah." Natalya moved back to her seat. "I've been thinking about it, too."

"I think we messed up the code. But I do think if we refine it and do some more work, we can get it to work."

She sighed. "But what we really need are more of those cubes so we can test it out first." She hated the idea of Reed and the rest of Hell Squad heading into danger to do something that might not work. Again.

"Well," Shaw said, his tone smug. "If that's all you need, you'll be happy to hear that I snatched a few on that last mission."

Natalya froze. "What?"

Shaw finished chewing, swallowed. "Grabbed half a dozen of those suckers as we were bugging out. Thought they might come in handy."

She jumped to her feet, leaned over to the sniper, and smacked a huge kiss on his cheek. "You are amazing."

He grinned. "Oh, well, I know. Next time I'll have to grab even more alien cubes. Then maybe you'll toss the SEAL over for a real soldier."

Reed made a growling noise and she looked over. He didn't look happy. With a smile, she walked back to him, framed his rugged face with her palms and pressed a kiss to his lips.

The quick kiss she'd intended swiftly turned hot, as he captured her lips with his. Before she could catch her breath, he yanked her into his lap. The entire dining room disappeared. It was only her and this man that saw through to the real heart of her.

"Get a room." Shaw's laughing voice permeated the haze. "There are kids present, you know."

Natalya pulled back and saw Shaw had his hand over a giggling Bryony's eyes.

"Cruz is always kissing Santha," the girl said.

Cruz laughed and Santha shook her head.

"Kid, seal it," Cruz said, chuckling.

As the others all laughed, Natalya pressed her forehead to Reed's and lowered her voice. "I can make that cube work." She could prove to everyone that she wasn't a raptor spy.

His hands came down over hers. "You have nothing to prove to anyone," he said darkly.

Her mouth dropped open. "Are you reading my mind?"

"No. You just have the most expressive face I've ever seen."

A communicator beeped and Natalya settled back into Reed's lap. She saw Santha open her device.

Suddenly, the woman sat bolt upright. "What? Where are you?"

Everyone at the table went silent, watching her intently.

"You're *where*?" She looked at Cruz, Marcus, then the rest of the table. "It's Devlin. He says he's found thousands of the raptor energy cubes."

Natalya gasped and the men around the table cursed.

"Where?" Natalya asked.

Santha's face turned dark. "On the alien spaceship."

Now there was shocked silence.

Marcus stood, his chair scraping on the floor. "He's on their spaceship?"

Santha nodded. "Yes."

***

Reed stared at the screen. The feed wasn't great, the image jumping around and filled with static. But he could see Devlin and he could see the strange room he was standing in.

Jesus, the guy was *in* the alien ship. He had to have a big brass set of balls.

Reed, Natalya and the rest of Hell Squad were crammed into Hell Squad's conference room in the Ops Area.

General Holmes had also arrived. For once, he wasn't in uniform, just wearing chinos and a white shirt. He looked...almost human. But the look on his face as he watched the screen was pure military.

Devlin was walking through a room on the alien ship. The walls made Reed think of the orange dome of the Genesis Facility that he and Hell Squad had blown to smithereens. The walls were the same amber color with black vein-like striations. Every now and then the walls pulsed with light. It was eerie as hell.

"The cubes are in here." Devlin's crisp voice was a little distorted.

"Can you clear up the image and audio?" Marcus asked Elle.

She was tapping on a comp screen, Noah hanging over her shoulder. "I'm trying." Elle pushed back a strand of dark hair with a huff. "But nothing's working. Something on the ship must be interfering with the signal."

"I'd like to know how the hell Devlin waltzed right into their ship?" Shaw said. "Right past who knows how many fucking aliens."

Devlin walked through an arched doorway. The next room was completely different. The walls were an oily-black and in the center of the floor was a huge stack of energy cubes, higher than Devlin's head.

"There are adjoining rooms just like this one." He panned the camera around. "Filled with these things. All operational."

"They must power the ship," Noah said.

"I think so," Devlin agreed. "And everything they do in here. Hang on, I want to show you the next room."

He passed through another doorway.

Reed wondered where the hell the raptors were. Security in the ship was pretty lax. Then again, it was tight outside and they probably never believed anyone would make it through undetected.

In the next room were cages. They were filled with animals from Earth. Birds squawked, monkeys screeched and somewhere a wolf gave a mournful howl.

"Fuck me," Claudia said.

"This isn't what I wanted you to see." Devlin kept walking.

Something in the man's tone made Reed tense. Whatever was coming wasn't good.

The next room was long and cavernous. It made Reed think of a manufacturing plant. A huge raptor-version of an overhead crane dominated the roof, looking like some giant black tentacle. On the floor, it looked like things were growing. They were circular, around half a meter high.

Reed narrowed his gaze. "Are those—?"

"They're making more genesis tanks?" Marcus said darkly. "Bastards."

"We have to stop this," Santha said. "Dev, how'd you get into the ship? Could you lead a team in?"

The image bobbled as the man turned the camera, his face filled the screen. "I came in from the water. They had loads of security and patrols on the land side of the ship, but they're clearly not expecting anybody from the ocean side."

Shit. Reed had seen the ship, resting on the old runways of Sydney airport. The airport was right up against Botany Bay. "We could infiltrate from the sea. Go in under the cover of darkness. Quickly and quietly."

"And we can plant the cube with the virus." Natalya was staring at the screen.

Reed's heart tripped. That meant she'd have to come on the mission. He *did not* want to take her there. Into the heart of the raptor territory, and into their fucking ship.

But as she turned and looked at him, he saw resolute determination. She wanted to do this. Maybe to prove herself, but also to strike back. And in the process, maybe heal the damage that had been done to her.

Damn. He released a long breath. *Damn.*

Suddenly the image whirled as Dev moved the camera. Throaty shouts came through the line.

"Shit." Dev started moving. "I've been spotted."

"Dev." Santha's jaw tightened. "Get out of there."

"I'll get to—" The feed cut off, leaving a black screen.

"Get him back," Santha demanded.

Elle's fingers flew over her comp screen. But after a moment, she sat back and shook her head. "I can't. He's gone."

"Can we go in and rescue him?" Reed asked.

Holmes' face was impassive. "No. I can't approve it."

Santha started to say something but Holmes shook his head.

"I'm sorry, but the majority of the raptor forces are located right on top of him. And more are within a short distance. If I send a team in, it's a suicide mission."

Santha ran a hand through her hair. "The idiot shouldn't even be there. He wasn't supposed to infiltrate their ship."

Holmes gave her a tight smile. "Get used to having people on your team who don't follow your orders." He arched a brow at Marcus.

Hell Squad's leader crossed his muscular arms and met Holmes' gaze, looking like he didn't give a shit.

"So there's nothing we can do?" Natalya asked quietly.

Reed slid an arm across her shoulders. "He's tough and damned good. All we can do is wait."

Santha's communicator beeped. She held it up, frowning, then she relaxed. "He got out." She laughed. "He sent me a message. He got out and he'll be home in a few hours."

"Crazy bastard," Reed said.

Natalya straightened. "We have to destroy those cubes. That'll leave them without the energy they need to manufacture more tanks." Her gaze landed on Noah. "Can you help me? I know we can get this virus working, and with the extra cubes Shaw snatched, we can test it out first."

"You got it," the tech genius replied.

Marcus faced his squad. "Meanwhile, we'll get started on an infiltration plan." His blue gaze fell on Reed. "You're our water man. I could use your help on this."

Reed nodded, his arm tightening on Natalya. Looked like he was going to hell again and taking his woman with him.

Chapter Thirteen

As the boat hit a small wave, Natalya gripped the edge of her seat. She was with Hell Squad and they were flying along the water, parallel to the shore. The long, narrow boat was soundless and fast. They hit another wave, salty spray bathing her face, and her stomach turned over.

Cruz stood at the front, operating the controls, with Devlin by his side guiding him in. Two lines of seats filled the back of the craft.

Reed was seated in front of her, just a broad, black shadow, but the sight of his strong shoulders made her smile. The rest of Hell Squad surrounded her. She was surprisingly calm. She could do this.

She pulled the cube out of the bag at her waist and turned it over. She and Noah had also programmed a second, backup one that also sat in the bag. She could sneak into the heart of raptor territory, plant the cube, and get out.

She looked toward the shore and saw the faint crescent of a white sand beach. Sydney had been well-known for its beautiful beaches. People would have flocked to the golden sand and waves on the weekends—either locals escaping the city or tourists soaking up the sun. She'd loved the beach and been one of the many vying for a patch of sand.

A few decades back, the pollution had gotten so bad that some days they used to close the beaches entirely. Then some tech company had used nanotechnology to create nanos that neutralized the water pollution, and the crowds had once again happily splashed, shown off their bikini bodies, and caught waves on their surfboards.

But now the beaches were empty and silent. No kids building sandcastles, or teenage boys spying on pretty girls. No tourists turning lobster-red under the strong Australian sun.

She sighed, her thoughts a bittersweet sting. But they were tempered by Reed's words. They had to look forward. If they could get these aliens to leave them alone, then maybe she could wear that black bikini on the beach one day in the future. Watch Reed rise up out of the waves, watch Bryony and the other kids from the base running and playing on the sand.

She dragged in a deep breath. But first, they had to find a way to beat the aliens...the bigger, badder and better-equipped aliens.

Just focus on the mission, Natalya. One step at a time.

"You okay?"

It was a near-soundless whisper from the man beside her. Roth Masters was the head of Squad Nine, but Marcus had roped him in to help with this mission. He was also a dark shadow in the night, but she knew he had rugged features, and sandy hair, and was built just like the men of Hell

Squad. Big and muscular. His squad was mostly women, and Nine was known for their impeccable timing as backup in a firefight.

She nodded. "Thoughts are whirling."

"Look up," he said.

"What?" She frowned.

"Up," he said again.

She did…and saw the stars.

"See that long tail of stars there, right above us? That's the constellation of Scorpio."

She spotted it. "And that red star?" It glowed a little brighter, was distinctly red.

"Antares. Heart of the scorpion."

"It's pretty." She smiled. "Thanks for the distraction."

"Don't let everything crowd in. Sometimes you need to clear your mind, and then focus on one thing at a time." Roth nodded toward her hands. "You just think of getting that in place. We'll get you there. MacKinnon will move heaven and earth to keep you safe, and then we'll show these aliens not to mess with us."

She turned the cube over in her hands. She and Noah had made numerous adjustments and tested the cube time after time.

They knew the virus would work this time.

They just had to get it in place, first.

The boat rounded the headland and into Botany Bay. For the first time since it had appeared in the sky over Sydney so long ago, Natalya saw the alien ship.

Oh, God. Bile rose. There were white and red

lights on all around it. She saw figures moving around on the ground—raptor patrols.

But it was the ship itself that captured all her horrified attention. It was huge. It looked like some giant sea creature, crouched there, ready to dive into the water and attack.

How the hell were they going to get in there without being seen?

Now her gaze strayed to the head of the boat. Devlin stood straight and still beside Cruz. He'd made it in and out, and he was here to lead Hell Squad back in.

She glanced up at the stars again and then slipped the cube into the bag on her belt. Time to show the aliens she wasn't just a damn guinea pig. A hand grabbed hers. Reed was still looking ahead, but he'd reached back. She smiled. God, she was so lucky he'd appeared in her life. At the darkest moment, her light had appeared in the form of six-foot-two-inch Reed MacKinnon.

They cut the engines and slid slowly toward the shore.

The boat stopped twenty meters out. "Everyone out," Marcus whispered. "I've dropped a micro-anchor and line to tether the boat out here. Don't want the raptors finding it on the shore."

Everyone in the boat stirred, readying to head overboard.

"And remember, we won't be able to contact base," Marcus said, tapping his earpiece. "We can talk to each other, but we can't send a signal out to Elle and risk the aliens detecting it."

Everyone nodded. Reed turned. "Here." He held something out to Natalya.

She took the tiny device. It was a small piece of metal with a mouthpiece.

"It's a breather. Just slip it in your mouth and it'll provide short bursts of air."

She eyed the shore. "But it's not far."

"Just in case. And don't forget your night-vision lens." He helped her flick the small lens from the side of her helmet and over her left eye. He leaned down and pressed a kiss to her cheek. "Be careful." Another kiss to her nose. "No risks." A light kiss on her mouth. "Stay by my side."

Her eyes fluttered closed. How could he pull her in, touch her soul the way he did, with just featherlight touches?

A kiss to her right eyelid. "You get hurt—" a kiss just under her right eye "—and I'll kill every raptor I can get my hands on."

Her eyes shot open. He looked dead serious. "Same goes, Reed. You get hurt, I'll make sure you only get cold water in your quarters for the rest of your life."

His lips quirked. "Deal. Ready?"

No. Yes. She was going to see this through to the end. She nodded. She watched him slip over the side and heard the others following. Natalya eyed the dark waters, tinged green by the night vision, and pulled a face. *Just think of your night swims with Reed.*

"Natalya." His face appeared at the edge of the boat. "Come on, brown-eyed girl. It's only a short swim to shore."

She climbed over, feeling far more awkward than Reed had looked with his easy flex of muscles. They were wearing modified, aquatic armor. It was more flexible, but less durable than the regular armor. It kept most of the water out, but the cool trickle that seeped through in a couple of spots made her swallow a gasp. Not too cold or shocking, but cool enough to feel it.

"Let's go," Marcus said quietly.

Natalya swam forward, following Reed. She saw the rest of the team ahead, they were staying low, just their heads visible above the water.

The shore got closer and she strangely felt herself steady even more. Sure, the alien ship ahead was scary, but their mission meant that other people might not suffer like she had in that raptor lab. That others wouldn't end up turning into the enemy.

Reed was right. She couldn't go back and be sharp, confident Dr. Vasin. But looking at him now, seeing him in his element, she didn't want to go back. She could be a new Natalya and Reed was a major part of that new life.

A splash to her left made her glance over. She didn't see anything, just a ripple in the water. A fish, maybe. She swallowed. *Please don't be a shark.*

Ahead, she watched as some of the others reached the shore and ran, hunched over, into cover. She realized her chest was aching. The water obviously didn't agree with her. She decided when this was all over, she was going to get Emerson to remove her scar.

Another splash and this time she felt something bump against her legs. Panic shot through her. God, there really was something in the water.

"Reed," she whispered furiously.

"Nearly there," he called back over his shoulder.

"There's something in the water."

"What?" With two powerful kicks he was by her side. "Keep quiet and keep moving."

She put all her energy into it. She wanted out of the water. Visions of big sharks and sharp teeth spurred her on.

Suddenly, a commotion in the water behind her made her gasp.

"Fucking hell!"

It was Shaw.

She spun, saw Reed doing the same.

"What the hell?" Reed breathed.

Shaw was being jerked around in the water and was thumping...something...with the butt of his carbine.

Shark. She shook her head, her lungs constricting. Then the animal reared out of the water.

Oh. God.

Everything in Natalya froze. *Not a shark. Worse than a shark.* The creature was huge. It had a long body, bigger than their boat, covered in dark scales and a long ridge of spikes right along its back. Shaw was twisting, trying to hit it with his weapon. Sharp teeth were clamped into his armor, holding him tight.

"Let him go." Claudia swam right toward the dinosaur-like, aquatic alien. The moonlight glinted off the huge knife in her hand.

She drove the knife into the creature's side, making it thrash, but it didn't let go of its prey.

"Goddammit." Marcus powered past Natalya and Reed. "Hell Squad, get that fucker off Shaw. Knives only. We don't want to use lasers and bring all the raptors down on us."

"Stay back." Reed touched her shoulder.

"Should I head to shore?"

"There might be more. Just stay still." Then he was gone, his strong kicks carrying him toward the alien.

She saw the team converge. Claudia was dodging the creature's flailing tail and it still clutched Shaw in what Natalya could now see was a vicious-looking mouth.

Reed and Marcus joined Claudia, stabbing at the animal. It let out a wild screech that made Natalya's heart stop. What if the raptors heard?

She glanced back toward the shore, but didn't see any movement. She knew Cruz and Gabe had to be there somewhere, worried.

The water around the creature churned as it thrashed. Then with a final screech, it dove into the water, taking Shaw with it.

"No, goddammit." Claudia turned in a circle. She slapped a hand on the water. "No."

"Look." Reed pointed. Several meters away, a

body bobbed up to the surface, hanging facedown in the water.

Claudia powered over. "Shaw!"

God, Natalya hoped he was okay. She kicked a little to keep afloat.

A ripple in the water ahead caught her gaze, made her chest constrict. *Oh, no.*

She saw a large spine rise out of the water, those spikes spearing into the air. The beast was slicing toward her.

A scream trapped in her throat. She wanted to swim in a mad rush to the shore, but she knew she wouldn't be fast enough.

"Natalya!"

Reed's frantic voice reached her. He'd seen the creature coming and was swimming in her direction.

She pulled out the knife he'd given her, tried to still her shaking hand.

And she waited.

The creature reared up as it neared her, and she saw an elongated face, jaws filled with ragged teeth, and two large eyes the size of dinner plates. They were fixated on her.

With the force of a runaway car, the alien rammed into her, snatching her in its mouth. She wanted to scream but she couldn't breathe. She felt its teeth digging into her armor, and terror almost made her drop the knife. Instead, she thought of Reed. The future.

She jammed her boot down on a tooth and pushed upward.

She couldn't quite reach. She pushed again, felt something tear and felt the prick of something sharp on the skin of her ribs.

But she gained the precious few inches she needed. It was enough. She jammed the knife into the monster's eye.

It let her go. She fell several meters to the water and hit with a splash. The creature dove, and the force of it rushing past her pushed her under the surface. Water rushed into her mouth and she tumbled, head over heels.

God, she couldn't breathe. Everything was black, and she had no idea which was up. Or if the alien would come back again.

She fumbled on her belt and snatched off the breather Reed had given her. She slammed it onto her mouth and pulled in a deep breath. Air. Precious air. She let herself float for a minute, and then kicked as hard as she could.

Her head broke the surface. She spat out the breather and gulped in air.

"Natalya. God." Reed appeared and dragged her into his arms. Then he was powering toward shore, towing her with him.

He pulled her out of the water and carried her up the beach several paces, until he fell to his knees. He yanked her to his chest, holding her tight.

"You're okay?"

She managed a nod, her fingers digging into his armor.

His hands ran over her. Her head, her face, her

body. "You're sure?"

"Yes." A croaky whisper. "God, I was so afraid."

"When I saw it grab you, I was terrified. Then it dragged you under." His voice broke and he pulled her close again.

She just held on and breathed him in until her pulse finally started to slow.

She heard voices and lifted her head. Marcus and Claudia were dragging a lifeless Shaw from the water.

They laid him down and Claudia knelt beside him. "He's not breathing." She looked up. "Who's got the resus kit?"

"Cruz?" Marcus pressed a finger to his ear. "Where are you? Shaw got attacked, we need the resus kit."

"Coming," Cruz answered. "We had to hide when a raptor patrol got too close."

Claudia tilted Shaw's head back. "Dammit, Shaw, you are never quiet like this, so talk, you cocky bastard." She pressed her mouth to his and breathed.

The sniper's hands reached up and gripped Claudia's head, holding her to him as his lips moved against hers. Startled, Claudia pulled back. "Shaw?"

"Damn, you have the softest lips, Frost. Never would have guessed it."

He sounded perfectly fine to Natalya.

"Damn you." Claudia punched him in the gut. "You were faking."

"Just got fucking beaten up and drowned by

some sea monster, Frost. That's not faking."

She smacked him again, and he grunted, but this time it looked like the woman's hit lacked power.

"Enough." Marcus grabbed Shaw's hand and helped him up. "If you've had enough of dancing with the wildlife, we need to join Cruz and Gabe. We still have a raptor ship to infiltrate."

Chapter Fourteen

Reed held on tight to Natalya's hand. He didn't want to let her go. Watching that alien creature take her... Reed barely had his shaking hands under control. It had been the fucking worst moment of his life. He just wanted to pack her back into the boat and get out of there.

But they had a mission. And even after the ordeal she'd just faced, she was staring ahead, shoulders back.

So much courage. He smiled, and together they moved with the team, sticking to the shadows and following Devlin toward the spaceship.

It was slow going. They used what they could for cover and avoided the small duos and trios of raptors patrolling the area. Sometimes they had to lie flat on the ground as ptero ships flew nearby.

But soon, the alien ship reared up above them, a towering black hulk.

Fuck. It was huge. Devlin led them right alongside it.

Finally, he stopped. He touched the side of the ship...and his arm disappeared.

What the hell? Through his night-vision lens, Reed could just make out where Devlin was touching was a lighter-colored patch on the ship. It was a dark gray compared to the ship's matte-black hull that looked like it was made of scales.

"It's some sort of membrane," Devlin murmured. "It covers an exhaust shaft that leads into the heart of the ship. We have to crawl in."

Great. Just fucking great. Reed sucked in a breath. Nothing he loved more than climbing through a tight space. Natalya's hand slipped into his. She looked like she knew just what was running through his mind.

"All right. Devlin will lead the way," Marcus ordered. "I'll go next. Then Gabe, Roth, Natalya, Reed. Claudia and Shaw, you bring up the rear."

Devlin squeezed through the membrane and disappeared into the ship. Marcus followed, then Gabe and Roth.

"You're up," Reed said to Natalya. "I'll be right behind you."

Claudia leaned around him. "That way he'll get to watch your ass the entire time." She grinned. "And I'll get to watch his mighty fine one. Hope you don't mind, it'll be in a purely objective, feminine way."

Natalya smiled, took a deep breath, then climbed through the membrane. Reed shook his head at Claudia. He knew she was just trying to keep Natalya calm. With a small salute, he crouched and slipped inside.

It was dark, even with his night vision. The narrow tunnel was barely wide enough for his shoulders. Damn, Gabe had to be feeling the pinch.

The sides were slick and just a little spongy. It was odd. He'd never seen anything like it before.

"Ugh," Natalya said from in front of him.

"What?"

"Nothing important. I just have...unidentified goo on my gloves."

He frowned. "Is it burning?"

"No, Reed." Amusement in her voice. "Nothing to worry about. It's just gross."

He grinned and they kept moving steadily. The tunnel turned a little, then took on an upward gradient. A few times, Natalya slipped and he caught her. After a while, it leveled out.

Finally, Roth turned back to them. "The others have dropped down through a hole. It's covered by a membrane like the entrance. I'll go down, and Natalya, I'll be waiting to catch you."

"Got it," she said.

Peering around Natalya, Reed just made out Roth as he swung down into the hole.

Natalya gripped the edge, determination on her face, then lowered herself into it. Reed watched her drop and Roth catch her.

A second later, he jumped through, landing in a crouch.

The room they'd landed in was filled with...they looked almost like eggs made of an amber-colored glass that reminded him of the Genesis Facility.

"We've seen this before," Marcus said, staring at the dome-covered beds. "This is where the raptors sleep."

"Really?" Natalya moved closer to one.

Reed heard the curiosity in her voice. Ever the scientist.

She peered through the amber cover, then jerked back. "Oh, God, there's a raptor in there." Her voice was a frantic whisper.

Reed grabbed her arm and pulled her back into the tight group of the team.

"Devlin, let's not hang around here," Marcus suggested.

The man nodded. "This way."

The squad moved in a tight formation, guns up. They followed Devlin down a long, curved hall. The walls were black but a glowing orange light pulsed through them.

Suddenly, Gabe went stiff. "Raptors. Headed this way."

Everyone froze. A second later, Reed heard it. The distant sounds of footsteps and raspy raptor voices.

Shit. He looked around. There was nowhere to hide here. No doorways. Nothing for cover.

He pushed Natalya behind him. They stayed there, frozen, ready to fight.

Then the sounds slowly faded.

"Keep moving." Marcus murmured.

Devlin led them into the cube room he'd shown them on the camera. Natalya gasped and hurried over to the stack of cubes. They towered over her head, all blinking on and off.

"Reed, watch Natalya." Marcus indicated with his head. "Everyone else, secure the exits. No one in or out."

Reed watched Natalya work. A crease furrowed her brow as she studied the cubes. She pulled one of her cubes out and clicked it into place, then she looked at her analyzer. All that focused concentration. He was so proud of her. Coming here was her worst nightmare, but there was no sign of nerves at being in the center of an alien spaceship. She was nobody's victim.

Then she cursed under her breath and looked up. Her brown eyes were troubled. "It's not working."

Reed sensed the others tense.

"It should work." She shook her head. "But nothing's happening."

"Stay calm." He edged closer. "You had it working back at base, right? You said it neutralized the other cubes you tested it with. Come on, use that exceptional brain of yours. I know you can work it out."

She released a long breath. "The tests worked perfectly. I know the virus is fine. So...it must not be interfacing with these cubes properly."

"Why wouldn't it work here?"

"I don't know," she bit out. She turned and stared at the mountain of cubes. "Something here is stopping it." Her gaze traveled over everything in the room. "I don't see anything—"

Her voice cut off.

Reed followed her gaze. "What? What do you see?"

"That." She moved forward.

Reed saw what looked like a small, black comp

screen on a stand. It was connected to the cubes.

She reached out, hesitated for a second, then pressed her palm to the screen. It flared to life and she snatched her hand back. She held up her analyzer.

"This is it." Excitement in her voice. "It's some sort of…authorization panel." Her face fell. "Oh, no, Reed. We need a raptor to do this."

Raptor symbols—they looked like claw scratches and gouges—appeared on the screen in a bright-gold color.

Natalya shook her head. "I don't know any raptor. Elle's the expert, right? And we can't contact her."

There were a few muttered curses behind them.

"Maybe you do," Reed suggested carefully.

Natalya turned her head slowly to face him. "I don't even remember speaking the raptor before, Reed. It wasn't a conscious thing. I certainly can't read any of this." She banged a fist against the screen.

Reed cupped her shoulders, hated that the armor hid her skin from him. "So stop thinking." He lifted her right hand, tugged off her glove, and gently placed her palm on the screen. "Just feel."

She closed her eyes.

The screen flashed, and then her fingers were moving, touching various symbols.

There was a deep beep. Natalya snatched her hand back, and pressed into Reed's chest.

The lights on the nearest cube to Natalya's, flickered…then blinked off. Slowly, the surrounding cubes did the same.

"It's working!" She pressed her hand to her mouth. "The virus is spreading, slowly but surely."

"You did it." He spun her and yanked her up for a quick kiss.

She was grinning.

Marcus came over. "Well done, Natalya." He eyed the cubes. "Looks like it'll take a while to spread to all the cubes. Devlin tells me there are more in the rooms connected to this one. Five rooms in total."

"The process should speed up as the virus replicates exponentially." Natalya watched the dying lights. "But the raptors will figure out something is wrong soon. We can't let them stop it."

"Okay, Hell Squad." Marcus swiveled. "We need to make sure no raptors get to these cubes before the virus finishes its job. Stay alert."

Once all the cubes had turned black, they moved into the next room. The virus was already well into killing the next set of cubes.

Hell Squad was tense, waiting at the doors, staring down their sights, ready for anything. Reed knew the aliens would come. It was only a matter of time.

The waiting was agony. It seemed to take forever for the lights on the cubes to wink out.

Finally, they moved into the final room. And their luck ran out.

"They're coming," Gabe said.

Reed couldn't hear anything but didn't doubt the other man's uncanny hearing.

Marcus settled against a doorway with his carbine. "All right, Hell Squad, let's do what we do best. Ready to go to hell?"

"Hell, yeah." Their war cry was murmured, but no less powerful. "The devil needs an ass-kicking."

Reed waited at his assigned doorway. Natalya was crouched by the cubes with as much cover as she could find.

Raptors poured down the corridor, their boots pounding on the floor, their weapons firing their burning poison.

Hell Squad opened fire.

The aliens kept coming and Hell Squad kept shooting. Claudia lobbed a grenade. It exploded, filling the hall with flames, smoke and screaming raptors.

Suddenly, a body appeared beside Reed, shooting. Natalya.

She held her laser pistol gripped exactly how he'd taught her. And her face had the same, steady look he'd seen on many soldiers in the field.

"Shit, watch out for the floor!" Roth yelled through the comms.

Reed swiveled and saw parts of the floor were opening and closing in the room. Trapdoors. One opened and a part of the pile of cubes poured down through it.

Another opened nearby and Gabe leapt off it just in time.

Reed gripped Natalya's arm. "Watch out—"

The floor opened up beneath them and they fell.

Chapter Fifteen

Natalya hit the ground, her hip taking the brunt of her fall. Pain shot through her. She heard the slap of Reed's body hitting beside her.

She was a little dazed, but he jumped to his feet and pulled her up.

"Anything broken?" he asked.

She shook her head. She squinted through the darkness. It was some sort of storage area beneath the room above. Organic raptor pipes and cables snaked along the walls and the floor. Fallen cubes were scattered around like giant dice.

Then she heard the grunts. She stepped backward, bumping into Reed.

He shoved her behind him and lifted his carbine. Three large raptor soldiers stepped out of the darkness, their red eyes glowing.

Reed fired. "Get down!"

Natalya obeyed and scuttled backward. She watched Reed kill one raptor, but the other two were on him. The fight was so fast, bodies whirling, fists hitting flesh, she couldn't work out what was going on.

Then she saw Reed tumbling, wrestling with one of the raptors. They slammed into a wall and then were rolling again, each fighting for supremacy.

That was when Natalya saw two black boots appear in front of her.

She looked up—way up—at the third raptor. His teeth were bared, his gaze fixed on her.

A shiver ran through her, but she forced her fear away. She was done cowering. She stood. Her hand fumbled on her belt, but her laser pistol was gone. She must have lost it in the fall. Her hand touched the second cube. She pulled it out. It wasn't much of a weapon...unless...

The raptor snorted and she lifted her chin. "You should have left us alone."

As she spoke the raptor language, the raptor's eyes widened. "You are...Gizzida?"

She shook her head. "I am not one of you. I'm human and we will fight for what is ours. Our lives, our planet." She lifted the cube, its red lights casting a glow on her hands and the raptor's scaled chest. "And I'll fight for the man I love."

The raptor moved, swinging his weapon up. But Natalya sprung forward and jammed the cube against the raptor's neck.

She leapt backward, watching as red electricity ran over the alien's body. He jolted, his eyes wide, a gurgling sound coming from his throat. Then he collapsed.

Reed staggered toward her. He was holding his combat knife and it was covered in blood. "You all right?"

She eyed the raptor she'd just killed. "Yes. I think I am."

Reed pulled her close. "You got a scratch on your cheek." He rubbed at it. "I heard you speak to it. What did you say?"

"That I'd fight for my life, my planet...my man."

His lips quirked. "I'm your man, huh?"

She gripped his neck and yanked his face down to hers. "You are, Reed MacKinnon. You're not getting away now."

"I have no intention of going anywhere." He shifted her to his side. "Come on. Let's get back upstairs and find the others."

They didn't find any stairs, but they did find some stringy ropes hanging down from an opening to the upper level. Reed shimmied up like a pro, but it took Natalya a little longer. Then they followed the sounds of battle to rejoin Hell Squad.

The fighting was fierce in the cube room. Raptor poison and laser fire was everywhere, creating sizzling patches on the ground and scorched burn marks on the wall.

She glanced at the cubes and saw they were almost all shut down. Her heart leapt. Three. Two. She watched the flickering lights on the final cube blink out. One.

The room plunged into darkness.

"Night vision!" Marcus called out. "And that's our cue to leave."

The night-vision lens helped, but Natalya had trouble making out who was who in the funny green shadows.

"Get back to the vent shaft." Marcus was already walking backward in the direction they'd come, but still firing into the corridor.

But when they all reached the doorway to the previous cube room, Natalya gasped.

More raptors were coming in. And this time, they had a pack of canids with them.

"Shit," Reed muttered. "We're cut off."

"Get this door closed," Roth called out.

Someone found the switch and the door slammed closed. Then the team fired on the control panel.

What were they going to do? If they couldn't make it back to the vent shaft...? Natalya wasn't going back into raptor captivity, that was for sure. And she had too much to live for to die in this damn alien ship.

Then a strange, high-pitched sound echoed through the room. Something darted in from the corridor, moving fast. The creature leapt up on the pile of inactive cubes, sending dozens scattering across the room.

Natalya swallowed, felt all of Hell Squad tense.

She'd never seen one, but knew what it was. Knew that it was a vicious, cunning killer.

Shaped much like the velociraptor dinosaurs of the past, it had clawed feet and an agile, strong body.

A velox.

"Damn." Marcus fired his carbine. "We need a way out. Devlin?

"I've got nothing," Devlin said. "We're stuck."

***

Roth

Things were not looking good. Roth Masters looked at the small comp screen strapped to his wrist. They needed a way out. Fast.

He really did not fancy getting gnawed on by alien dinosaurs.

In front of him, he watched Hell Squad take down the velox.

But he knew more of the damn things would be on their way. And whatever other nasties the aliens had here on their ship. He suspected they hadn't seen everything, yet.

A map of the ship appeared and he tapped the screen. It wasn't complete. When they'd first entered the vessel, he'd set off an experimental mini-drone. It wasn't much bigger than a bee and was busy buzzing its way through the place, taking scans as it went.

In a break in the firing, he caught Marcus' gaze. The other man's face was hard as stone, his scar stark against his tan skin.

"I think I have a way out." Roth tipped his arm to show the map. "We can go down through one of these trapdoors."

"It was just storage down there," Reed said.

"But it looks like there's an area of offices—or whatever the raptor equivalent is—adjoining it."

"Incoming," someone yelled.

Everyone turned to fire at the raptors dumb enough to try to storm the door.

"If the map's right," Roth continued. "There's what looks like a window in this office." A way out.

"It'll be a hell of a drop, Masters," Marcus said.

Roth raised a brow. "A rough landing or become raptor bait."

"I guess a jump is better than what we've got," Marcus grumbled. "Let's move, Hell Squad. Masters is taking the lead."

Roth sprinted for the nearest hole in the floor and jumped down. His boots hit the ground and he rolled, then leapt back on his feet.

He heard some of the others drop down after him.

"Masters?" Reed called out.

Roth moved under the hole. "Toss her down."

Reed lowered Natalya and Roth snatched her out of the air.

"Thanks," she said.

He set her down and gave her a once-over. She was staying calm and steady. He approved. MacKinnon dropped down beside them and pulled her to his side. Roth mentally nodded. MacKinnon was a hell of a soldier and he sure as hell deserved a woman who looked at him like Natalya did.

"MacKinnon, you up for setting a few booby-traps?" Roth gave the man a thin smile. "Slow down anyone who follows us?" He knew Reed was an expert with explosives.

Reed looked at Marcus, who nodded. Then Reed grabbed something off his belt. "Sure thing."

Once Reed had finished, Roth waved everyone on. "This way." He led them through a door, following the directions from his partial map.

Steele ran a tight squad, but Roth missed his own team. He knew they'd be pacing back at base, bitching about not being part of the action. He got a lot of ribbing about having a mostly female team, but they were some of the best soldiers he'd ever worked with.

And damn, women could be smart and cunning. He'd learned a thing or two from them.

The next room was the office. Desk-like platforms were lined up with raptor comp screens on them.

Everything was dark and empty.

Natalya touched a screen and it came to life. She snatched her hand back.

"Thought there was no power?" Shaw said.

"There must be a failsafe," Natalya said. "Some sort of emergency backup so they don't lose their data."

Raptor data might be useful. Roth slipped a small metallic hacker device from his pocket. He slapped it onto the edge of the desk and activated it. Its tiny illusion system triggered and the hacker blended into the desk.

"What the hell is that?" Marcus demanded.

"A little bit of tech Noah asked me to test out. Same as the mini-drone. The hacker will collect whatever data it can from the raptors' system, and if we send a drone in range, it can download whatever the hacker has stored."

"How come I don't have anything like this?" Marcus said with a scowl.

"You must not have asked nicely." Roth smiled. "And I think Noah used to have a thing for Elle until you stole her out from his lab. Maybe he hasn't forgiven you?"

Marcus' scowl deepened. But when the hacker emitted a tiny beep, Roth frowned.

"Shit, it's having trouble interfacing to the computers." He looked at Natalya. "I hate to ask, but can you open the raptor comp system so I can sync the hacker with it?"

Something moved through her eyes, but she nodded. "I'll try." She touched the screen, her fingers moving over the raptor symbols.

"The window is over here," Devlin called out from the other side of the room. "I'll see if I can get it open."

"I'll help," Claudia said.

Roth checked the hacker. "That's it. Operational. Thanks, Natalya." He glanced at the screen covered in raptor scrawl. Then he noticed some English. The word Negotiation. Frowning, he tapped it.

Information filled the screen. Pages of what looked like classified Coalition government documents.

One file with a photo on it caught his eye. His mouth snapped shut, his jaw tight. The person in the photo looked very familiar.

He read the name. Special Agent Avery Stillman.

He reared back. In the photo she looked all spit and polish, with a serious face and almond-shaped, hazel eyes. When he'd pulled her from a tank in the

Genesis Facility, her dark hair had been long and bedraggled, and there'd been nothing polished about her. He could hardly forget her, though, since she'd attacked him like a wild pitbull. She'd landed a few good hits while he'd been trying to subdue her without hurting her. He'd had to get the doc to heal his black eye after.

"Window's open," Devlin called out. "Time to go."

Roth cleared the raptor screen, but the image of the woman was burned into his brain. Clearly, there was a lot more to Special Agent Stillman than just being an alien lab survivor.

Roth had more than a few questions for her.

And he always got his answers. One way or another.

Chapter Sixteen

Natalya gripped the frame of the window. "I can't jump out of here. It's too far." The ground looked a very long way away.

"You can," Reed said calmly. "Or you can go back the way we came."

She pulled a face at him. "I won't survive that fall."

"The exoskeleton in your armor will do most of the work. Here, watch Claudia."

The female soldier shot Natalya a wink, climbed up on the edge of the window and leapt out. When she reached the bottom, she crouched to absorb the impact, then was up and running into cover. She made it look easy.

Natalya pulled in a breath. The raptors would find them soon. She had to do this.

"Just think, after a short boat ride and a quick trip in a Hawk, you can have a nice, long shower back at base." He gripped the back of her neck and his voice lowered. "I'll make it worth your while."

"You'd better." She climbed up on the ledge. "On three, okay?"

He smiled. "One. Two." He pushed her.

Natalya fell, waving her arms in the air and

swallowing a scream. It felt like the longest drop ever, but then her feet hit the ground.

The landing rattled her teeth and she ended up on her knees. Nothing like Claudia's neat maneuver. But she was out of the ship, and not hurt.

Reed landed beside her, bending his knees. She pushed herself up and as they hurried into cover, she slapped his chest. "Asshole."

His chuckle made her want to hit him again. "You can punish me later."

She didn't miss the sensual promise behind his words.

Marcus and Roth followed behind them and soon the entire squad was huddled behind a stack of raptor supplies.

Not far away, raptor troops were mobilizing. Groups of them were manning large search lights. They were swinging them around the area surrounding the ship.

"How the hell are we going to get back to the boat?" Shaw asked. "They'll spot us in a second."

"I think I can help." Roth pulled an item from the backpack on his back. It was the size of a tennis ball and metallic silver.

"More gadgets." Marcus shook his head. "What is it?"

"A portable illusion system."

"For people?" Marcus asked, surprise clear in his voice.

"So the geeks say."

"I'm having a long damn chat with Kim when we

get back. I want some of this experimental shit."

Roth depressed the button on top of the device. A hazy shimmer surrounded them. "We have to stick together and move slowly. Too fast, and the illusion fails. Anyone too far from the device will be visible. Its range is only a few meters."

They all huddled together and Natalya found herself in the center of a group of huge, muscled soldiers. They shuffled away from the cover, heading for the beach.

Her heart was a loud thump in her ears. Not long now. Soon, they'd be far away from here.

"Stop," Roth whispered.

A raptor patrol crossed ten meters in front of them.

"Go."

"Nearly there," Reed whispered.

Natalya could see the beach and the water ahead. She let out a breath.

Just then, a lone raptor appeared out of the shadows.

Three meters from them.

They froze.

God, it was heading in their direction. Natalya's lungs clogged. She willed the alien to turn, to go somewhere—anywhere—else.

The alien strolled closer. Dammit, he was going to walk right into them. She felt the tension coiling in Reed and the others.

A shout sounded from the alien ship. The raptor stopped and looked.

High up on the ship, she could just make out

raptors yelling from a window. The window Hell Squad had leapt from. The raptor in front of them turned and took off at a sprint.

Natalya released the breath she'd been holding.

Their group moved a little quicker now. Soon, she felt sand under her boots.

"Illusion is off," Roth said.

"Who fancies a swim?" Reed asked, eying the water.

Natalya's stomach cramped. She did *not* want to go back in the water. The surface was smooth, calm, with no signs of the giant alien creature, but in her head the Jaws theme was playing.

Da-da. Da-da.

"Let's just get the fuck out of here." Marcus strode into the water. "The sea monster can go to hell. I just want to get home to my woman."

Natalya waded in beside Reed. Every meter felt like a kilometer. Adrenaline was surging through her system, leaving her jumpy and breathless.

They reached the boat and Reed helped her in. A minute later, they were racing away from the ship.

They'd made it. She quivered. They'd gone into the alien ship, destroyed the energy cubes and made it out in one piece.

"Look!" someone said.

Natalya's pulse spiked, and she glanced back.

The lights on and around the ship were shutting down. One by one, the search lights blinked out. Raptors were yelling, their shouts echoing across the water as they were plunged into darkness.

"Hot damn," Shaw said. "Now that is a pretty sight."

Reed slid an arm around Natalya's shoulders. "Well done, my brown-eyed girl."

His words made her feel good. She knew she wasn't a victim anymore. She rested her head against him. He felt good, too. Really good. She was a fighter and now she had something to fight for.

***

Reed whistled as he strolled through the tunnel heading to the comp lab. A full day had passed since their mission to the alien ship. During the last twenty-four hours, there'd been no raptor patrols in the city, no pteros in the skies, no rexes rampaging through the suburbs.

Peace and silence. Almost like the alien invasion had never happened.

General Holmes had been sending extra scavenging teams out to hunt for supplies, and also teams to search for any holed-up survivors.

Reed knew the aliens wouldn't roll over easily. They were no doubt in their ship, regrouping. But he would take what he could get, and he planned to take his sexy scientist swimming at their pool. In the sunshine. Maybe make love to her in the grass.

He grinned. She'd really messed those scaled bastards up. He was damned proud of her. The aliens wouldn't be growing any more genesis tanks...at least not for a long time.

Reed saw the comp lab door ahead. Now, he

wasn't going to think about raptors for the next few hours. He had a beautiful woman to see and—he patted his pocket—a question to ask her.

In the lab doorway, he stopped and watched her. She was scribbling on a tablet, her brow creased in concentration, and she had her glasses on. Reed gave a mental groan. She looked so sexy.

"Hey there," he said.

She raised her head and her face lit up. She pushed her chair away from her desk. "Hi, yourself."

Damn, she was wearing one of her skirts. This one was navy-blue with a faint stripe through it. He strolled over to her and dropped a kiss on her lips. "What's got you holed up in here?"

Her smile widened. "I think I can get us twenty-four-hour-a-day hot water!" She bounced in her chair.

He shook his head. "You and your hot water."

"I've spliced some alien tech into the power system. Some of it from the alien glass from the tanks and some from the energy cubes. I still need to do a few more tests…but I know it will work. It's good to be able to put something of theirs—something ugly—to a good use. Human ingenuity with a touch of raptor."

Reed cupped her face. "Perfect. And just like you." He rubbed a thumb over her lips. "Human with a touch of raptor."

She pulled a face. "I think I've accepted it now. I'm not defined by one organ." She rubbed her chest. "And I think I'll get Emerson to remove my scar." She smiled. "Then I'll wear that bikini for you."

"Don't remove it for me." He moved her fingers aside and touched her scar. "I don't care about it at all."

"I know." Her hand covered his. "But I think I'll remove it for me. It's time to move forward."

His fingers flexed. "Good. And with or without that scar, I love you."

Her mouth opened. "What?"

"I love you, Natalya Vasin. And I have something to ask you." He got down on one knee, and when he saw her huge brown eyes go wide, he almost smiled. But now, a touch of nerves was making his gut tight. He cleared his throat. "My parents were older when they had me, so some of the values they instilled in me are a little old-fashioned. Like getting down on one knee when you ask the woman you love to marry you."

Natalya opened her mouth, closed it, then bit her lip.

He pulled the box from his pocket and opened it. The diamond twinkled under the lab lights. He'd used all his trading credits and borrowed a few from his squadmates to get the ring from the small selection of jewelry the clothing store carried.

"Natalya, will you marry me?"

"Oh my God, Reed." Her voice was jerky.

"Is that a yes?"

She reached for the ring, then hesitated. "Are you sure? I don't have my heart anymore, but if I did, I'd give it to you."

Jesus, she could burrow deep inside and touch every part of him. "I'm sure."

A single tear rolled down her cheek, but she was smiling. "I love you, too. And I'd be honored to be the wife of the toughest, sexiest, bravest man I know."

Elation slammed through him, stronger than all the times he'd come home from a successful mission. He slipped the ring on her finger, then leaned forward and kissed her.

Her hands slid into his hair and jerked him closer. The kiss went from sweet to hot in a blink. She moaned into his mouth, her tongue dancing with his.

Then he was surging upright. He plucked her out of her chair, turned, and set her on her desk. Her tablet crashed to the floor.

His hands were on her skirt, yanking it up to her hips. He reached down and in one swipe, tore her panties off her.

She gasped. "Reed!"

"I can't wait, sweetheart."

"Someone might come in."

"Door's locked. And I told Noah I needed some time with you. To propose. I didn't mention this exactly, but we won't be interrupted." Reed delved between her legs, loving the husky cry she made. She was so damn beautiful.

"Now, Dr. Vasin, I want to tell you about this librarian fantasy you've sparked in me."

She peered down her nose, her glasses slipping a little. "Oh? Did you forget to return a library book?"

He growled and captured her mouth again.

He'd always fought for freedom. Always wanted his own and thought that meant wide-open spaces. He'd just never realized he'd find it in Natalya's arms. No matter where he was, with her, he'd always have his freedom and his fresh air.

I hope you enjoyed Reed and Natalya's story!

Hell Squad continues with ROTH, the story of Squad Nine's tough leader. Coming Sept/Oct 2015.

Don't miss out! For updates about new releases, action romance info, free books, and other fun stuff, sign up for my VIP mailing list and get your free copy of the Phoenix Adventures novella, *On a Cyborg Planet.*

Visit here to get started:

www.annahackettbooks.com

FREE DOWNLOAD

JOIN THE ACTION-PACKED ADVENTURE!

Formats: Kindle, ePub, PDF

Read the first chapter of At Star's End

Book 1 of the Phoenix Adventures

READY FOR ANOTHER?

**ACTION
ADVENTURE
TREASURE HUNTS
SEXY SCI-FI ROMANCE**

Dr. Eos Rai has spent a lifetime dedicated to her mother's dream of finding the long-lost *Mona Lisa*. When Eos uncovers tantalizing evidence of Star's End—the last known location of the masterpiece—she's shocked when her employer, the Galactic Institute of Historic Preservation, refuses to back her expedition. Left with no choice, Eos must trust the most notorious treasure hunter in the galaxy, a man she finds infuriating, annoying and far too tempting.

Dathan Phoenix can sniff out relics at a stellar mile. With his brothers by his side, he takes the adventures that suit him and refuses to become a lazy, bitter failure like their father. When the gorgeous Eos Rai comes looking to hire him, he knows she's trouble, but he's lured into a hunt that turns into a wild and dangerous adventure. As Eos and Dathan are pushed to their limits, they discover treasure isn't the only thing they're drawn to...but how will their desire survive when Dathan demands the *Mona Lisa* as his payment?

Dr. Eos Rai gripped the edge of her seat and gritted her teeth. The pilot of her hired minishuttle executed a dizzying spiral descent toward the moon below.

The free fall was exactly what her life was like at the moment. Her hand clenched on the seat. How much longer until she hit the bottom?

Eos focused on the irregular, pockmarked surface below. Her first look at Khan.

The moon was a captured asteroid that now orbited the market planet of Souk. If she craned her neck, she could just make out the large planet with its urban areas interspaced with farms and forests.

Here at the edge of the known galaxy, Souk was the stopping-off point for explorers, colonists and daredevils heading off into unknown space to make their fortunes. And its small moon of Khan was home to the most notorious treasure hunters in the galaxy—the Phoenix Brothers.

Another sharp turn and she almost head-butted the synth-glass windshield. She shot a narrow look at the pilot, but the weathered old man peered straight ahead through his thick glasses—who still wore glasses when you could visit a medbooth and get your vision fixed for a few e‑creds?—didn't even glance at her. In fact, he looked bored.

As long as she landed in one piece...

She had to make the Phoenix brothers help her.

She pulled in a deep breath and rubbed the fingers of her left hand together. She felt the slight bump at the end of her index finger and thought of the precious cargo it carried.

It challenged all her beliefs to put this into the hands of treasure hunters, but she was out of options.

She'd worked with Niklas years ago at the Galactic Institute for Historical Preservation. He was steady and smart. She trusted him. His brothers, though, were the wild cards.

Why the hell had Niklas thrown away a promising career in astro‑archeology for this? She stared at the scratched and dinted hulls of the various starships that littered the moon's surface. A spaceship graveyard.

But she knew it wasn't the brothers' main business. No, they went after items far more lucrative than scrap metal.

Dathan Phoenix had a reputation for sniffing out the choicest ancient relics.

Right or wrong, it was a skill she needed. *If* she could convince him to chase a myth.

He was legendary across the Exodus quadrant. Not to mention cursed in the halls of the Institute.

Heat seared under her rib cage. Artifacts that should be in vaults or museums, taken by his grubby hands and then sold to the highest bidder. Her mother had died trying to keep artifacts out of the hands of pirates.

Eos smoothed a finger over the floral markings that traced up the back of her hand and twined around her wrist. The familiar habit soothed her. No one had the right to steal someone's history.

"There she is," the pilot said.

Eos's gaze shifted downward. A large huma-dome shimmered pink-purple on the horizon. The energy field of the dome kept the atmosphere inside but also permitted solid objects to pass through. Moments later, the bubble-shaped shuttle shot straight downward—along with Eos's stomach. The light lunch she'd had earlier at the spacedock on Souk threatened to come back up. The shuttle descended through the dome and touched down on a small landing pad.

"Thank you." Eos didn't hide her eagerness to exit the shuttle. She'd already transferred payment into the pilot's account before the trip, leaving her e-cred account dangerously low. Her stomach clenched. She'd already forked out a small fortune for the commercial fare to get to Souk. What she had left was to convince the Phoenix brothers to help her.

As Eos slipped on her small backpack, the shuttle shot upward, bathing her in steam. Spinning, she faced the building.

No one to greet her.

Hmm, security sucked. Her boots made a quiet tap on the smooth floor as she headed inside the monstrous warehouse.

The inside was packed with...junk. Mostly ships—or parts of them—of all types and sizes. She spied lights in one corner of the building and wended her way through the debris.

As she passed a small pile of rusted metal, she glimpsed paintwork on the...whatever it was. She stopped and crouched, smoothing a hand over the surface.

"It can't be," she breathed.

NASA was written in faded white paint, with a small flag made up of stars and stripes. Remnants of a Terran satellite!

She shot to her feet. So little was known about the world that had seeded life on so many planets in the galaxy. Most of the planet's records had been lost after its nuclear devastation in the Great Terran War. She imagined for a second what it must have been like with the world's superpowers at war. Even over the name of the planet itself. Earth had been the English term used by the United Countries of the Americas, but the records showed that in the other powerful group of countries, the Northern Federation, they'd used Terra. Both terms were now commonly used throughout the galaxy.

Eos's mouth firmed. This satellite should be in a museum being studied, not rotting here on a desolate moon. She marched toward the back of the warehouse. The light she'd spotted was spilling from a half-open door. She pushed it open.

Living quarters. Not tidy ones. She noted the clothes strewn across the floor. A large bed with rumpled covers was pushed against one wall. A battered metal desk was closest to her.

What sat on it had the breath rushing out of her lungs.

She circled the desk. "By Suva's grace." A Renaissance bronze in mint condition. She'd only ever seen pictures of them in records. She reached out a trembling hand.

Then she was yanked backward.

A strong arm wrapped around her chest like a steel band. A hard male body pressed against her back. She stiffened and shoved her elbow into a firm abdomen. A wet, naked abdomen. The cool metal of a weapon pressed against her temple and she froze.

"I've already had one woman sneak up on me today. I don't plan to make it two." The male voice was low, raspy.

"I don't care what kind of day you're having." She wasn't violent by nature but she'd been trained to defend herself on isolated digs. Acting on instinct, she dropped low and swiped out at his ankles with her foot.

She obviously surprised him, because he toppled. Pulling her over with him.

For a second, she glimpsed the lean, tough body of a runner—all firm, sinewy muscle. She had a quick impression of dark ink covering one of his arms. She didn't let her gaze go lower.

He was strong and she realized she'd never beat him in a fair fight.

He was cursing in a language her lingual implant didn't recognize. She scrambled off him, reaching for the laser pistol that was now lying on the floor.

Her fingers brushed metal. Then she was tackled from behind.

She hit the floor face-first and all the air was forced out of her lungs in rush. The man's heavy weight settled over her and her cheek pressed against the smooth concrete.

Warm breath tickled her ear. "Now what, darlin'?"

"Now nothing. Get *off* me." Eos bucked her body. But all that did was grind her butt into a hard stomach.

"Not until you tell me who you are and what the hell you're doing in my place."

She sucked in a breath. "No one met my shuttle."

Footsteps.

"Her name's Dr. Eos Rai."

Eos recognized Niklas's voice. Relief flooded through her. She turned her head enough to see Niklas and a younger man with tawny hair in the doorway.

The younger man smiled. "Twice in one day you've gotten beaten up by a girl, Dath."

"Screw you, Z," the man above her said.

She guessed the one with Niklas was the former Galactic Strike Wing fighter pilot, Zayn. Which left the hard, dangerous man on top of her as none other than Dathan Phoenix.

His weight shifted off her and she sat up.

Now she knew who he was, she let herself look.

Tanned skin over hard muscles. Actually, he was a bit pink, like he had bad solarburn. Not that it detracted from his blatant masculinity. A washboard stomach and a deep V of muscle that disappeared...downward. Where she wasn't going to look.

One strong arm and shoulder were covered in black ink. Her heart stuttered as her gaze traced the wild, masculine design. She pressed her hands together, touching her own designs. His markings were nothing like the elegant mehndi markings the men and women on her world were born with.

Dathan grabbed a towel off a nearby chair and wrapped it around his hips, then he crossed his arms over his chest. Her gaze met eyes the color of the bright blue-green mountain lakes on her home world. Hair the color of deepest space fell around a slightly battered face and a small white scar cut through his left eyebrow.

"How are you, Eos?"

She forced her gaze away from Dathan. "Niklas. It's nice to see you."

"So you know each other?" Dathan asked with a frown.

Niklas nodded. "We worked together at the Galactic Institute of Historical Preservation."

Dathan's face tightened. "We're not real fond of Institute snobs around here."

She arched a brow. "I'm on a leave of absence." A forced one, but they didn't need to know that.

Dathan extended a hand, his intense eyes burning through her. "Well, regardless of your profession, I'm sorry about the gun in your face. Like I said, it's been a rough day."

She put her hand in his. Ignored the tingle where their palms met. "Spent in the sun?"

He rubbed a hand over his stubble-covered cheek and she thought the color in his face deepened. "Something like that."

"This is the last place I'd expected to see you, Eos," Niklas said.

She lifted her chin, forcing her mind off the distracting treasure hunter beside her. "I need your help. I want to hire you." She let her gaze move over them. "All of you."

The brothers traded a quick glance. She marveled at the fact that such a quick look and they all seemed to understand each other. Some sort of sibling shorthand.

"Let me get dressed." Dathan strode to an adjoining room. "Why don't you guys take the doctor to the living area?"

The living area was section of the warehouse adjacent to the bedrooms. Lived-in furniture was clustered around a bank of large screens. A tiny kitchen was tucked against one wall.

Zayn called out a command and the screens flickered to life—showcasing the latest sporting craze, VelocityBall. Eos was not a fan of the new version of football with a powered ball. Niklas sat in a leather armchair and she watched him extend the superthin palm-sized Sync communicator until it was tablet size. He flicked at information on the clear touchscreen while Zayn prowled to a nearby cold unit and plucked out a drink. He glanced her way. "Want one?"

Eos shook her head. "No, thank you." She wandered to a window. Through the glass, she saw the shimmer of the huma-dome. "Pretty interesting setup you have here."

"We do what we can," Niklas said.

She'd had a taste of what it was like without the Institute's large resources this last week. "You miss your work at the Institute?"

"No."

She sensed...something. "Why did you leave?"

Something stirred in his dark blue eyes. "Dathan needed me. Our father had died and...it was time to come home."

She cast an eye across the cavernous warehouse. "You have pieces in here that should be in museums. Pieces we could learn so much from."

Footsteps.

"Locked away for the rich and educated to admire? Gathering dust in some storeroom somewhere?"

She turned. Dathan looked just as good clothed.

Worn jeans hung low and his white shirt was unbuttoned, giving glimpses of that sculpted chest. His ink was hidden, though, and she was sorry she couldn't see it.

She looked away. It was dangerous to stare at

him. Dathan Phoenix wasn't just legendary for his treasure hunting. "In the hands of people who will ensure their proper preservation." She wanted to reinforce the galactic laws, but she needed to hire these men, not alienate them. She bit her lip instead.

Dathan shoved his damp hair back and raised an eyebrow. "Yet I'm guessing since you want to hire us, you need us to take something for you?"

He had her there. Her jaw locked. No, she was nothing like this man. "Yes."

"You going to share, darlin'?"

"It's Dr. Rai."

Niklas coughed. Or maybe laughed. "Eos is one of the foremost experts on Terran artifacts."

"You won't get us anywhere near Earth," Dathan said. "No one who goes there ever comes back."

Eos longed to explore Earth, but she knew the radiation levels from the nuclear fallout of the Terran War were off the scale. Besides, rumors were that *something* had survived down there...and it didn't welcome visitors.

"I'm not after Earth." She lifted her chin. *Okay, here goes.* "I need you to help me find the last remaining piece of da Vinci's *Mona Lisa.*"

Silence.

All she could hear was the gentle whoosh of the internal environmental system. It made her nerves stretch tight.

Dathan threw his head back and laughed.

"I'm serious," she snapped.

He shook his head. "We only take jobs that have a sure payout. The *Mona Lisa* was destroyed when Earth's inhabitants turned their planet into a nuclear wasteland."

"No. It's at Star's End."

Dathan laughed again, grabbing his stomach. Eos felt a burning urge to kick him.

"Star's End is a myth," he choked out.

Zayn leaned back against the wall, popping a piece of gum into his mouth. "Legend. Fable. Fairy tale." He blew another bubble.

Niklas shook his head. "Star's End and the Lost Treasure of the New Louvre have become so muddled with pseudohistory and garbage no one can be certain it's even real. No one really believes the director of the New Louvre sent the museum's most precious treasures on an expedition to set up a distant colony."

"It makes sense," Eos insisted. "Earth was on the brink of destruction. The United Countries of the Americas and the Northern Federation were decimating the planet in their bitter war. Lots of people were leaving Earth with the hope of finding habitable planets to set up new colonies, to make new homes. What better way to preserve the Earth's greatest historical treasures?"

Dathan shifted. "It's the Holy Grail of the crazy." He tilted his head. "You crazy, Dr. Rai?"

"No."

He stalked closer, circling her. "What's a fine upstanding astro-archeologist like you doing searching for something that could ruin your career?"

He was getting too close. "Finding the last fragment of the *Mona Lisa* would be a crowning achievement."

Niklas leaned forward in his chair. "The Institute thinks the expedition never left Earth."

"My research indicates otherwise."

Dathan watched her. Silent. Like a predator.

"I found a journal." Well, partial records of a journal but they didn't need to know all the detail. "Written by the daughter of one of the head colonists. She didn't want him to go."

"Maybe he never did."

Eos held his gaze. "She talks about how much she missed him."

"Plenty of Star's End hoaxes out there." Dathan shrugged. "I think I have a record of a man who opened the first strip club at Star's End."

She ground her teeth. "I've seen an archived document from the New Louvre that shows they packaged the last known fragment of the *Mona Lisa* ready for transport. It was loaded onto the starship *New Hope,* which was headed for Star's End."

Silence again.

She knew it was big.

Dathan raised a brow. "You're telling me you have a verified document that links the New Louvre to Star's End?"

She huffed out a breath. "No. I couldn't take it—"

"I didn't think so."

"I've heard of the document," Niklas said. "Institute ruled it a hoax. The last fragment of da Vinci's masterpiece perished when Paris was nuked at the beginning of the Great Terran War."

"It isn't a fake." God, they were her last hope. She knew it'd be a hard sell, but she didn't think treasure hunters would be worried about verification of documents.

"Didn't your mother work on the original authentication?" Niklas asked.

"Yes." Dr. Asha Rai had been one of the Institute's most talented. "She never believed it was a fake but bowed to pressure from her team. That belief led to her death."

"How?" Dathan asked.

Eos felt the familiar tightness of grief. "She went on an expedition to find Star's End. She was killed by space pirates."

Dathan leaned closer and her chest tightened. "I'm really sorry about your mother, but do you really want us to scour the galaxy searching for a mythical old Earth colony?"

She smelled him now. Some citrus-scented soap and warm male. "I hear you're very good at finding things."

They stared at each other.

Zayn snorted, breaking the moment. "Not so good at holding on to them, though."

Dathan flashed his brother a narrow look before he turned back to Eos. He caught her chin. "Why isn't the Institute backing you?"

Oh, she really didn't want to go there. She tried to jerk away from his touch. "They don't have enough evidence—"

"I want the truth, Doc. You smell a little of desperation."

Her spine stiffened. "It's an old promise I intend to keep and the Institute isn't interested. Now, do you want to hear what other information I have or not?"

His eyes narrowed and he moved closer. His chest brushed against her. "Not really. This is already more trouble than it's worth."

"I can pay you."

One dark brow rose. "How much?"

She thought of the last e-creds in her account. It was more than most people saved in a lifetime, but she knew it was no fortune. "Five million."

He snorted. "Not enough to tempt me."

Eos *had* to convince him. "I have more information that helps narrow down the location."

His gaze was so sharp it felt like it cut through her skin. "I'm listening."

She shook her head, ignoring the heat coming off him. "I won't tell you until you agree to take the job."

"That's asking for a lot of trust, darlin'." Dathan stepped closer still. They were plastered against each other.

Something told her he was seeing what would make her back away. She stayed where she was and lifted her chin. "I guess trust isn't a commodity you have in abundance."

Those intense eyes burned through her.

"You can trust us, Eos," Niklas said.

She shook her head. "Trust the most notorious treasure hunters in the galaxy? Not with Star's End and a Da Vinci relic worth a trillion e-creds."

Dathan's grip on Eos's jaw tightened, the rough calluses on his fingertips abrading her skin. She felt like he was staring straight inside her.

"You have a location," he said.

She swallowed. Heard Niklas's chair squeak and saw Zayn straighten behind Dathan.

"Look at me."

She obeyed, caught again by those eyes.

"You know the location of Star's End, don't you?"

"Yes."

The Phoenix Adventures

At Star's End
In the Devil's Nebula
On a Rogue Planet
Beneath a Trojan Moon
Beyond Galaxy's Edge
On a Cyborg Planet

Also by Anna Hackett

Hell Squad
Marcus
Cruz
Gabe
Reed

The Anomaly Series
Time Thief
Mind Raider
Soul Stealer
Salvation

Perma Series
Winter Fusion

The WindKeepers Series
Wind Kissed, Fire Bound
Taken by the South Wind
Tempting the West Wind
Defying the North Wind
Claiming the East Wind

Standalone Titles
Savage Dragon
Hunter's Surrender
One Night with the Wolf

Anthologies
A Galactic Holiday
Moonlight (UK only)
Vampire Hunter (UK only)
Awakening the Dragon (UK Only)

About the Author

I'm passionate about ***action romance***. I love stories that combine the thrill of falling in love with the excitement of action, danger and adventure. I'm a sucker for that moment when the team is walking in slow motion, shoulder-to-shoulder heading off into battle. I write about people overcoming unbeatable odds and achieving seemingly impossible goals. I like to believe it's possible for all of us to do the same.

My books are mixture of action, adventure and sexy romance and they're recommended for anyone who enjoys fast-paced stories where the boy wins the girl at the end (or sometimes the girl wins the boy!)

For release dates, action romance info, free books, and other fun stuff, sign up for the latest news here:

Website: AnnaHackettBooks.com

Printed in Great Britain
by Amazon

36185849R00117